Hexes & Hijinks

The Chronicles of Addison Schmidt – Book Two

Cassidy K. O'Connor

Hexes & Hijinks

An Addison Schmidt Novel

Copyright ©2024

Published by: Celtic Hearts Press, LLC

Cover by: Crooked Sixpence Book Covers

Formatting by: Celtic Hearts Press, LLC

Groundhog familiars, an emotional-support witch, and ghosts who love drama. That is the everyday life of Addison Schmidt.

As shadows deepen and an ominous presence slithers forth, Addison finds herself at the heart of a supernatural storm. With a blend of curiosity and trepidation, she embarks on a journey, unearthing ancient curses and navigating the unpredictable currents of midlife romance.

As the line between magic and mundane blurs, Addison stands at the crossroads of fate, armed only with her groundhog confidante's sage advice and a healthy dose of beginner's luck.

In a tale brimming with humor, heart, and a touch of the otherworldly, Addison navigates the tangled web of destiny with equal parts grace and clumsiness.

one

ADDISON STARED at the envelope in her hands. This was it. The DNA results were in. Her mother, Theresa, had said she didn't want or need to hear anything a test had to say. Addison didn't blame her. She would give anything to roll back a month and forget everything she'd learned. She hadn't asked for perimenopause to kick in and unleash magical powers that she had zero control over. She'd always been klutzy, but the wayward magic had made everything worse. She'd lost so many kitchen appliances to fire and she'll never forget when she somehow managed to make a flamingo lawn ornament eight feet tall. The hijinks were never ending.

The letter was starting to wilt from her sweaty

hands. She didn't want to blow her family up. It had to be done though. If a whole line of Addison Schmidt's had come before her, she owed it to them to learn the truth.

She blew out a breath and ripped the envelope open. She silently read the results and then read them again.

Maybe she was misinterpreting something, so she read it a third time.

There it was, in black and white. Theresa was not her biological mother. So who was?

She felt so alone. Heat rushed through her body as nausea threatened to make her lose her breakfast.

"Hey Addison, the Netflix has paused again," Alexander shouted from the living room.

Well, not completely alone.

Francesca and Alexander were ghosts she'd met at the secret society meeting. They liked her so much they asked to come home with her. She'd accidentally shown them Netflix, and they'd been on a binge for days. Apparently, ghosts don't sleep.

She had tried to watch with them, but when they got to Bridgerton and Alexander nitpicked every little thing, she gave up. He wasn't British. How did he know exactly what it was like? She tried to argue the right to have creative license. That didn't work with him either.

She still had the letter in her hand when she went to the couch and pushed the button to have the show play again. "You know, when my kids were little, I made them play outside one hour for every two hours of video game and television time."

Francesca looked up from the TV. "What's wrong? You sound like something's wrong." She tilted her head and read the results. "Oh, honey. I'm so sorry."

There was a brief knock at the front door.

"Come on in." Minnie, Addison's emotional support witch, had texted she was on her way over with news. She was tasked with helping Addison get control of her magic. If Addison didn't, they would bind her magic and erase her memory. They deemed her a threat.

Rude.

Minnie breezed in. As always, she looked like she had just stepped off Madison Avenue with her red silk blouse and pencil skirt. How she walked in those four-inch heels was beyond Addison. "Morning everyone. Oh, season three is a good one." She turned and caught sight of Addison's face. "I'm guessing you got confirmation about what we already knew?"

Addison was still trying to get used to Minnie's sarcasm. "Something this big needed confirmation."

Minnie nodded. "Let's go in the kitchen so we don't disturb these two."

It didn't look like a bomb exploding would disturb the two ghosts. They were practically fused to the couch. Minnie glanced back at them. "I still can't believe John wins."

She laughed loudly as they shouted and cursed at her for ruining the surprise.

Addison loved the *Great British Bake Off* as much as the next person, but it was only a baking competition. There was no need to threaten to haunt Minnie for the rest of her days.

"Man, I love messing with them." Minnie sat down with a satisfied smile.

"That was cruel." Addison admonished her as she nuked two cups of coffee and then sat down. "I hope your news is better than mine was?"

Minnie smiled brightly. "Actually, it is. As you know, Marilyn came to a coven meeting the other night, and we weren't able to break the shroud over her. Whoever bound her magic and made her forget who she was had to be seriously powerful. Sonya talked to the Raydell coven and they've agreed to join with us to try again. They're a bigger and stronger coven. We'll unblock Marilyn and your mother, and then you can settle down and focus on your studies. It's not enough to be born into a magical family."

Addison ignored the jab. It wasn't her fault she came from a long line of insanely powerful witches.

"On that note, should we get some practice in?"

Addison glanced at the clock on the microwave. "Sure. I don't have a lot of time, though. It's Fitz's birthday and I still need to get his present sorted out."

Minnie rolled her eyes. "Children can be so time-consuming. Did you read the book on the elements?"

Fitz was twenty-eight, not exactly a child. Addison didn't have the energy to argue. She nodded. "Having the ghosts absorbed in the TV has given me lots of quiet time. I think I'm connected to the fire element, given I keep setting fires."

Minnie waved her hand and the space in front of Addison shimmered like something was coming into focus. Four objects appeared on the table. "Magic isn't always logical. It's not safe to assume anything. Let's see how you do with these. The feather is to test air, the seed for Earth, the candle for fire, and the glass of water is obviously for water."

The witch had the gall to back up against the counter and conjure a police riot shield. She looked ridiculous in her high-heels expecting the worst.

Addison lifted one eyebrow. "Really?"

Minnie shrugged. "I've seen what you can do. Better to be safe than sorry."

Emotional support witch probably wasn't the right term for Minnie. Addison had expected her to be kind and gentle. Minnie believed in a tough love kind of approach.

"Look at the four objects and start with whichever one is calling to you."

Addison nodded and took her time studying each item. Fire had to be her element. She stared at the wick, imagining it lighting. Her skin tingled, and she almost lost her concentration when she realized her nipples had hardened. That was new.

She cleared her mind again. Her intent was obvious. Maybe too obvious. There was a hint of smoke a second before a raging blast of fire shot up, almost reaching the ceiling, and melted the candle into a puddle of wax.

Minnie waved her hand and put out the fire.

"Are you trying to kill us? Didn't you know they stopped burning witches at the stake?" She shook her head like she was chastising a child. "Are any of the others calling to you?"

Addison stared at the glass of water. Her nipples hardened again. What the hell?

She meant to create a swirling tornado in the glass. Instead, the faucet turned on, and a stream of water stretched across the room and filled the cup to overflowing. She scooted back when the water ran over the table and toward the floor.

Minnie waved her hand again, and the chaos stopped. "Interesting. Anything else?"

For a minute, Addison stared at the seed. What was her intention supposed to be with that? Her nipples were almost painfully hard now.

In her mind, she pictured a small rose unfurling from it.

The little seed danced around like a kernel about to turn into popcorn when suddenly it split open. A rose grew out of it, along with ten more and vines which were snaking their way toward her. One of them wrapped around her wrist and another was going for her neck. While she struggled to get free, she saw Marilyn's roses out the window growing and heading right for her.

Minnie did her 'fix Addison's chaos' hand wave. "A little bloodthirsty, aren't you? Not sure what your intention was there."

Addison's hands were still around her throat, where the vine had started to choke her. "Really? You think I would intend for anything even remotely like that?"

"You are a strange woman whom I barely know. How am I supposed to know what you're thinking? Now, try the feather."

Addison crossed her arms to hide her perky nips and concentrated on making the feather lift gently into the air. She wilted in relief as it floated fancifully a few feet above the table. See, nothing bad happened.

A screech from the living room was her first indication something was wrong. Before she could get up to investigate, several pillows came flying into the room and landed on the table. Something was moving inside them. "I don't think I want to know what that is." A shudder racked her body as she pictured worms or snakes slithering in a big ball of horribleness.

Suddenly there was a ripping sound as small holes were made in the pillows. Feathers flew out and floated around the room.

Addison wilted against the chair. "Oh thank god. I was imagining so much worse."

"You do make a mess, don't you? Maybe that's why the coven sent me. I tend to be a little reckless myself."

Addison turned to say something snarky back. A snort-laugh escaped her before she covered her mouth. A majority of the feathers had flown at Minnie and were sticking to her. She looked like Big Bird's little sister.

"Oh no. I swear I didn't mean to do that." She wiped the tears from her eyes as Minnie shook the feathers off and sat down at the table.

"Well, it would seem you have a connection to all four elements. You may still have one stronger than the rest. We'll figure that out as we go." She tapped her nails on the table as she studied Addison. "I've never met anyone connected to more than two. Your family must be incredibly powerful."

Excitement coursed through Addison. If you're going to be a witch, why not be a super-powered one? What's the worst that could happen?

two

ADDISON FELT like the weight of the world was on her shoulders. She drove to Luna's shop *The Soul Apothecary* in a fog as she imagined several different ways she could have the conversation with her mother about not being her mother. Theresa insisted she didn't want to know the results. Addison wished she could honor her request. It just wasn't possible. She would not give up until she knew who her real family was. Theresa was going to need to be on board with that.

The little bell over the door of the shop rang as Addison walked in. The smile fell from her face when she saw Luna arguing with a man at the checkout counter. She'd never seen him before.

Luna's cheeks were flushed. Whatever the man was saying was pissing her off.

Addison tried to move out of view so she wouldn't interrupt, but ended up running into the section of wind chimes hanging up. The tinkling sound rang through the room, making Luna and the stranger look directly at her.

He rolled his eyes at her and turned back to Luna. "I'll win in the end. I always do." He looked quite impressive as he stormed toward the door. He reminded her of Dracula with his suit and cape. The fanciful and highly unrealistic item danced around him as he spun to glare at Luna one last time. "I would hate for anything bad to happen."

Addison gasped. If he was trying to give a veiled threat, he failed. It was obvious he meant harm to her new friend.

As the door closed behind the man, Luna collapsed onto the stool behind the counter. Her normally bouncy blond curls were flat and dejected looking like her.

Addison rushed over. "What the hell was that all about?"

Luna glanced up and blinked a few times to clear the tears from her eyes. "It's nothing. What can I do for you?"

"Are you sure you're okay?"

Luna gave her a droll look. "What do you think?" She growled.

Addison hated seeing her so upset. She knew exactly how to cheer her up. "I have a bit of a personal question and there's no way I'm asking Minnie."

Luna's eyes lit up. "Go on."

Addison took a deep breath. "Do your-" she waved her hand in front of her boobs, "-boobs react when you do magic?" She'll give her credit. Luna didn't laugh. She looked like she wanted to.

"Well, no, my boobs don't do anything when I cast. The bottoms of my feet tingle. I once knew a girl who farted every time she did."

Addison gasped. "Oh my god. That is so much worse than what's happening to me." They were silent a second before bursting into laughter. "We shouldn't be laughing." Addison sucked in a big gulp of air.

Luna nodded as she wiped the tears from her eyes. "You're right. The poor woman never did magic in front of anyone because of it. To expound on your question though, most witches have some physical reaction when they cast. It's part of your entire being connected physically, mentally, and psychically." She shrugged. "Sounds like a fun side effect to me. I have innies, hard nipples are difficult for me. I'd be happy to show them off. You could always get some of those breastfeeding pads for your bra to hide when it happens."

Was there no indignity perimenopause wasn't going to bring?

Luna shook like a wet dog trying to get the water off it. "That's better. I'm sorry about my mood. Forget all that. What brings you to the shop?"

Addison wanted to help. Luna was making it clear she didn't want it. When she was ready, Addison would be there for her. "Well, Fitz's birthday is coming up. He pretty much has everything he could ever want. I was thinking something magical might be fun."

"Is he the one that has the hots for your ghost houseguest?"

Addison sighed. "No, that would be my middle son, Leo. Fitz is my oldest and Iggy is my youngest. I still don't know what I'm going to do about Leo's crush. For now, it seems like it's not hurting anything and I am getting to see him more often since he's visiting Francesca all the time." She walked over and plopped into the chair by the table. "Of all the supernatural creatures he could have gotten smitten with, it had to be the one he couldn't have a real, physical relationship with. What's a mother supposed to feel about that?"

The bell over the door rang as two young girls in cheerleader outfits walked in. Luna held a finger up to Addison to wait. "Don't move or touch anything."

Geez. A few minor accidents and you're labeled as a bull in a china shop.

The girls wanted to learn about tarot cards. Luna pointed out the various decks she had and gave them a book on how to interpret the cards. She walked them by the incense and crystals, explaining how to use them to cleanse themselves before using the cards.

Addison had to respect Luna's smooth upselling tactics.

She walked them to the register but stopped them when the first girl tried to buy her own deck. "Some believe you shouldn't buy your own. You should always be given the set. I don't necessarily buy into that, as I believe you should buy the set you are drawn to. Since you're new to this, I wanted you to make your own choices."

The girls looked at each other and then giggled when they swapped decks. The blonde handed over her items. "I guess we're kind of following both. We picked out the deck we wanted and will buy each other's as a gift."

Addison smirked. She was a clever one.

Luna rang them up and handed over their bags. "If you ever find yourselves stuck with any interpretations, feel free to come in and I'll help you. In fact, I will be starting some classes on how to read tarot and a bunch of other fun stuff. Follow me on social media and make sure you tell all your friends."

The girls giggled and whispered to each other as they left.

Luna sat in the chair across from Addison. "They'll be back. There's not a lick of magic in either of them. I can sense their openness and eagerness, though. With practice, they'll be able to pick it up."

"I didn't know you were starting up classes. That sounds exciting. You can guarantee I'll be at every one of them. I have forty-six years to catch up on. What made you decide to start doing these?"

Luna stared into space for a few seconds. "It's what I love and I want to share that with as many people as I can while I can."

Addison didn't like the way she said that. What on earth had happened with that man?

"Plus, I've noticed around town people stare at me and whisper behind my back. I can feel how many of them are curious and want to come into the shop but are too afraid to. I thought starting some beginner classes might entice them in. Especially if I offer wine or soda in the case of those girls."

Addison snort-laughed. "That is very true."

Luna slapped the table in front of her. "Enough about me. What are you thinking for Fitz?"

"I was hoping you could help with that. I don't even know what's possible, so how do I choose?"

"Hmmm. Good point." She tapped her nails on the table as she looked around the room. "Does he like games of the mind? I can get the items together to make a magicked chess set. I have a friend who figured out how to make wizard chest boards like in Harry Potter. Best of all, if he has normies around, he can use a command that makes the board act like a normal one."

Addison gasped. "That would be incredible. I know he has played a few times. If the pieces move and attack like they did in the books, he'll definitely be eager to use it. The only problem I see now is not having his brothers get jealous."

They laughed at the absurdity of her boys fighting over the set. It'll be like they are twelve years old all over again. When Leo and Iggy's birthdays came around, she was going to have a high bar to reach to make sure their presents were as cool as Fitz's would be.

Finally, magic was bringing something good into her life. She could use a little less chaos.

A faint tippy-tapping sound behind them had both women turning to investigate. No one had come in, so there was no reason for the noise.

And then the damndest thing happened. A furry creature wearing a shirt and pants rounded the corner. "What's up, good looking?"

Addison screamed.

Luna screamed.

The creature screamed.

What fresh hell was this?

three

ADDISON STARED at the animal wearing clothes. The shifters they'd fought at the warehouse when Antony had been catnapped hadn't been wearing outfits. They didn't talk either. That could have been because they were spelled to kill them, though.

The bell over the door rang as two women walked in. Luna pulled Addison behind the counter and waved the animal over to join them.

"Why are we hiding?" The creature asked.

Luna's eyes bulged. "Because most of my customers are human, so I can't have a talking prairie dog, can I?"

He shrugged and hopped up on a low shelf so he was on eye level with them. "First of all, I'm a groundhog. It's offensive that you assume we're all the same. Second, my name is Nutmeg."

Luna and Addison looked at each other before bursting into laughter.

Nutmeg crossed his paws and scowled at them. "Is my name funny?"

Addison sobered immediately. "Not at all. You've caught us off guard, is all."

He seemed satisfied with her lame answer. "So, what are we doing today? Going anywhere fun?"

Addison glanced at Luna, hoping the animal was talking to her. No such luck. His tiny brown eyes were fixed on her. "I'm sorry, I would say who is we, do you have a mouse in your pocket? But that seems absurd. Your pockets are too tiny."

Luna shook her head at her.

She couldn't help the way her brain thought. "Why do you think you're hanging with me today?"

"Because I'm your familiar, of course." His chubby cheeks lifted as he smiled proudly.

Addison shook her head emphatically. "No thanks. I read about familiars. They seem great and all, but I'm not ready for that."

Luna patted her shoulder. "That's not really how it works. If he is your familiar, you'll be stronger with him than without."

"But I don't want him… no offense."

"Oh, I'm starting to take offense." Nutmeg shot back.

"Addison, is that you?"

Ugh. She knew that voice. The grating tone belonged to Augie Stilt, a nosy body who loved gossip. She came into the coffee shop every morning and talked to anyone she could, all while changing her order several times after it was already made.

Addison had begged Callie to ban the woman from the shop. Callie's answer was to not let Addison wait on the woman. It may also have something to do with Addison's accidental fires. They always seemed to happen when Augie was annoying her.

Addison stood up and pasted on her customer service smile. "Morning Mrs. Stilt."

The woman dragged her eyes up and down Addison. "Money must be tight if you are working here, too. You poor thing. Maybe you should make yourself more presentable and beg your husband to take you back."

Magic crackled in the air. Addison hadn't even realized it had come from her. She was a split second away from sending the baskets of crystals flying right into the gossip's face.

Luna hopped up and shoved Nutmeg into her arms. "Go, I'll take care of this."

As soon as Addison touched the animal, she felt the tiniest tendril of connection. Damn, he was her familiar. And she could feel how pissed he was at being woman handled.

Augie tried to lean around Luna as she shoved Addison toward the back of the store. "Was that a cat? Was it wearing clothes?"

Luna took a deep breath and turned to face the obnoxious woman. "Sorry about that. I'm Luna, and this is my shop. I can sense you're here because you need help with your husband. You're worried he's going to stray?"

Augie gasped and glanced around to make sure they were alone. "How- What-"

Luna steered the woman to the front corner of the store. Not before Addison caught a glimpse of tears in her eyes. It's why Addison always tried to be nice. People hid their struggles. Was that why Augie was so nasty?

Addison understood how it felt to be in a bad marriage.

She growled loudly.

Nutmeg snorted. "You actually feel sorry for that shrew?"

Addison set him on the counter and crossed her arms in a huff. "No. I'm starting to see why she is the way she is, though. That doesn't excuse her nastiness."

Nutmeg sat on the edge, his feet dangling over the side. "You think your husband had affairs."

Addison glared at him. "I'm already not liking this connection." She picked him up and spun around. "Come on, I'll take you to a park and you can be on your way."

"Has anyone ever told you how stubborn you are? You said you read about familiars, so that means you know we're in this together."

She turned the corner and passed a man who looked at her strangely. "Look, I'll take you with me, but can you lie in my arms like a baby?" His tiny jaw dropped open. "My life is chaos right now. I'm rarely wearing clean clothes, I set things on fire, and now I have ghosts living with me. I already look like a crazy lady. I'd like to not be the crazy lady who talks to chipmunks." She shrugged her sweater off and waited for him to give in.

"I'm a groundhog." He grumbled as he rolled onto his back and curled into her arm.

"Thank you."

"Mommy, look, she has a squirrel." A little girl

was running at Addison. Her mother was right on her heels.

"Olive, wait." The woman caught up and pulled Olive back against her. "I'm so sorry."

"But mommy, it's a squirrel, look." Olive's tiny hand reached upward, trying to peek inside the sweater. Her mother shoved it down.

"I'm so sorry about this. I'm Beth, this is Olive. I don't know what has gotten into her."

Thinking on the fly Addison cooed at Nutmeg. "It's okay, go back to sleep."

"I miss when Olive was that small. May I see him?" Beth leaned forward.

Addison quickly rolled Nutmeg into her chest. "Sorry, he's shy. I need to get him home for his nap. It was nice meeting you."

She rushed off as Olive stamped her foot. "Mommy, it was a squirrel, not a baby."

She was definitely living up to the crazy lady persona. Now all she needed was people whispering she was a witch and her role as town pariah would be complete.

four

ADDISON SAT in her mother's driveway, scared to get out of the car. If she drove away now and pretended the test had never happened, they could go back to the way things were.

Who was she kidding? You couldn't unring the bell.

Thanks to her familiar showing up, she was late meeting her mother. This conversation was too deep to do in front of Nutmeg, so she dropped him off at home with the ghosts. They were going to show him the latest show they were binging. If nothing else, they'd keep him busy.

The paper with the test results shook as she gripped it. She knocked and went inside. "Mom?"

"In the kitchen," Theresa called out from the back of the house.

Addison dragged her feet all the way to the small kitchen table and sat down sullenly. "Sorry I'm late."

Theresa brought over two cups of coffee. "It's okay. We don't have much time, though. Minnie is picking me up for that coven meeting."

"Shit. I completely forgot about that." She straightened the paper out and laid it on the table. "I might as well rip the band-aid off. We're not blood-related." Tears filled Theresa's eyes. Addison grabbed her hands. "You are my mother. Nothing will change that."

"I don't understand. How is this possible?" She got up and grabbed a book off the counter. "I've been studying your baby albums. You look like the baby I delivered. I don't think you were swapped. You have that cute birthmark on your right arm."

Addison flipped through the pages. Tears pooled in her eyes at the memories. There was a picture of her with her birthday cake every single year. She laughed at the pictures of the one time they'd gone camping and the disaster it had been. By the time they were home, they were soaking wet and covered in bug bites. The trips to the aquarium and zoo were all documented.

She'd had a good childhood. She'd been loved. This woman had been with her every birthday and every other holiday. Well, not every one. "Why are there no pictures before my first birthday? You don't have any pictures from when I was born?"

Theresa crinkled her brow as she glanced around. She grabbed the book from Addison and flipped through as if she was sure Addison had just missed them. "I guess those are in a different album. I hadn't even noticed they were missing."

It was a plausible explanation. In her gut, Addison knew that wasn't the reason why. Something happened in her first year of life. If Theresa truly didn't know, then that meant magic had to be involved.

A loud knock on the front door stopped her from spiraling. "Minnie's here."

Theresa cocked her head. "She'd be early. Are you sure?"

Addison shrugged and went back to staring at the pictures while Theresa went to answer the door. Minnie had helped her realize she could see a person's wavelength. Every person's was different, like their fingerprints. Once Addison memorized them, she could sense when that person was nearby.

Minnie's wavelength was a jumble of energy,

fluctuating up and down rapidly, all while exuding a sense of confidence.

"Isn't this a surprise? I came early because I thought you might be preoccupied with a new visitor, so I was going to bring your mom to the meeting." Minnie grabbed Addison's cup of coffee and drained it. She really did make herself at home. Addison would have made her cup if she'd just asked.

"New visitor?" Theresa asked as she sipped her own forgotten drink.

Addison sighed. "It turns out I have a familiar, and I can already tell he's going to be a handful. I already raised three energetic boys. Couldn't I have gotten like a sweet butterfly or something?"

Minnie washed the now empty cup in the sink. "You aren't raising him. He's older than you. And I wouldn't let him hear you talk like that. He looks small and unassuming, but he holds an immense amount of power. You don't want to be on his bad side."

Was that snarky little creature really older and more powerful than her? Maybe there was more to him than Addison first thought. "Should I bring him to the meeting? We can tap into his power?" If it helped break the block over Theresa and Marilyn, she would gladly do it.

"You haven't done the ceremony yet to bond with him. If you tried using him while we are casting an intense spell, it could cause all sorts of trouble."

"Ceremony? No one told me there was a ceremony. You guys really need a step-by-step guide. You can call it 'Being a Witch for Dummies'.

Minnie snorted. "Maybe you can write it as you learn. Most of us have been using our magic since birth. We aren't going to remember every little thing. Now, we don't want to be late for the meeting. It would be rude not to be there when the Raydell coven shows up."

A sliver of excitement coursed through Addison. She hadn't attended a coven meeting yet and now she was going to meet two at the same time. She'd been working really hard to calm her energy, so there wasn't a repeat of the secret society drama. Everyone had been so sensitive. Like she meant to insult five different kinds of paranormals within a twenty-minute period.

She knew more now. She'd walk in there with confidence and fake like she belonged with them.

The drive to the meeting had been tense. Minnie had offered to drive them and bring them back. Theresa was consumed with the news. She wasn't Addison's mom, and Addison was trying to control her nerves. Her understanding was a coven is your family. Her life would be better with them. She was determined to make a good impression.

They pulled up to a standalone building at the end of Main Street. *The Magic Kiln* had been around for years. Addison had taken her boys there to paint ceramics. She'd never known it belonged to a witch.

The sign on the door said 'Closed for Private Class'. Smart way to cover up their meetings.

Luna pulled up next to them and squealed as she caught up to them. "I got an invitation to attend the meeting. If all goes well, I'll be allowed to join." Her face changed to a pout. "And thanks for leaving me with that lady. Boy, was she a piece of work. It took me an hour and a half to get her out of my shop. Her husband is definitely cheating on her."

"So, what did you end up giving her?" Were love potions a real thing?

"Nothing big. A candle to light in his presence to help him see her better and some tea leaves she can have him drink that will help him remember why he loved her to begin with. The rest will be up to her."

Minnie nodded her head. "Good job. Some witches get way too invested in fixing the human's problems. You don't want to get a reputation as someone who can help you with anything. They'll never let you be. Especially in a small town like this."

The door was opened by a statuesque blonde. Addison hadn't seen her around town before. She would have remembered someone so gorgeous. "Evening everyone. Mariska asked me to bring you back."

As she turned to lead them, the smell of freshly baked brownies and the ground right before it rains filled the air.

Addison tripped over a table, sending the ceramic cups flying. The woman quickly stopped them with magic and righted the table.

Heat rushed to Addison's cheeks. "Sorry about that. You smell so good. I got a little distracted."

Luna nodded. "You do smell amazing, like lemons and roses."

Theresa shook her head. "No, she smells like lavender and whiskey."

All three argued until Minnie clucked her

tongue. "Really Constance. Stop messing with them."

The gorgeous blonde shrugged innocently. "You know I can't turn it off. I specialize in magic of the heart, endorphins, and sex."

"Coolest powers ever," Luna whispered in awe.

"You smell what your brain thinks are your favorite scents." Constance nudged Theresa. "Whiskey? Love it. You are a girl after my own heart. I do apologize though. I can usually dampen that endorphin trip, but I can't fully shut it off. I'm so excited about all the new guests tonight and I completely forgot."

Addison's eyes bulged. "I would never dampen that. It felt amazing. You need to figure out how to infuse that into candles. It would help a lot of depressed people out there."

Constance pursed her lips as she thought about it. "Interesting idea. I'll have to play around with that idea. More often than not, it's a hindrance though. It tends to make people think they're in love with me. You can imagine the ruckus that causes."

Addison didn't think she'd ever had anyone love her to the point it caused a ruckus, but she nodded in agreement anyway. Even now, when she looked back on her marriage, she could see that her husband hadn't loved her. She'd been a practical choice for him.

That was going to stop now. She would never settle for anything but absolute passion and devotion. She wanted to wake up every morning, eager to open her eyes and look at the man next to her in bed. She wanted him to struggle to fall asleep because he didn't want to be apart from her. The image of Xavier popped into her head.

Theresa grabbed Addison's arm and pulled her back. "Are you sure it's okay I'm here? I'm not in danger, right? Do I avoid looking into a vampire's eyes so they can't hypnotize me? If a fairy tries to give me something, should I refuse? I don't know the protocol and I'm kind of freaking out."

Addison hadn't thought that far ahead. Now that she mentioned it, Addison kind of wanted to know those answers, too. Surely if any of those old wives' tales were true, someone would have warned her ahead of time. She glanced over at Minnie. Would the saucy witch warn her?

Minnie noticed her staring. "What? Do I have something on my face?" She opened her phone's camera and checked her face. "Nope, everything is perfect. So why were you staring?"

Addison shrugged. "I wasn't intentionally. I was lost in thought, that's all."

"Well, be careful who you stare at in there. Some might get the wrong idea."

Before Addison could ask for more detail, a curtain in the back lifted.

The woman Addison recognized from her trips to the shop walked out. "Are we holding the meeting up here, or would you like to join us?"

"Sorry." Constance made an oopsie face and rushed past the older woman with chestnut hair and emerald green eyes.

There must have been a magical bubble around the room. As soon as they stepped through, they were inundated with voices. Men and women were spread around, talking animatedly. Several had their familiars with them. Addison felt a little bad about leaving Nutmeg behind.

Mariska walked to the center of the room and stood next to a woman with eyes that almost looked golden. It was a beautiful contrast to her dark skin.

The chairs were set in a circle around the two women. The room fell silent as everyone took a seat. Marilyn with Antony, her cat husband in her arms, waved at them before sitting.

"What an exciting night. We have our brothers

and sisters from Raydell with us, a few new witches to our coven, and of course, the main event where we'll try to break the spell shrouding a couple of them."

The woman next to her went next. "My name is Asha. I'm the High Priestess of the Raydell coven. We thank you for allowing us to right an old wrong by letting us handle the Malvado sisters. In return, we're happy to help in any way we can. We know how strong your coven is. If you aren't able to break the shroud, then it must be a very impressive piece of magic. We are eager to explore it."

Addison was very glad she wasn't the one with the block. She felt like they were looking at Theresa and Marilyn like they were specimens to be tested on.

Two men got up and put chairs in the center. Mariska walked over and held her hand out to Marilyn while Asha came and got Theresa.

Her mother looked at her with a fleeting moment of panic before Asha whispered something in her ear and she instantly calmed. Addison could have used that trick when her sons were little and acting up.

"This better not hurt." Antony's Scottish brogue

rang around the room, causing several people to chuckle.

"If at any time you want to stop, let us know and we will cease immediately," Mariska assured him. "Everyone gather close and hold hands. Focus on the shrouds covering these women and channel your intent into breaking them free."

Addison had butterflies in her stomach. This was her first group spell. She'd been getting much better at focusing her mind. She wouldn't be the weak link this time.

Candles set up around the room all lit at once. Addison's skin prickled as she felt the magic in the room building. Mariska and Asha took turns saying a spell. Addison jumped when everyone spoke up at the same time and repeated the chant, *The time has come, free the innocent and be done.*

Electricity coursed through her as she joined in. The power of forty witches and wizards flowed through her. Every cell in her body was lit. She felt like she could do anything.

Her mom's scared face caught her attention. She refocused on the intent and chanted with the rest. Their voices rose to a deafening level when an ear-piercing scream tore through the room.

Theresa was on the floor in a ball, sobbing. "My baby."

Addison broke from the group, fell to her knees next to her mother, and pulled her into her arms. "I'm here. What's wrong?'

Anguish rolled off of Theresa as she sobbed. Addison felt so helpless. She lifted tear-filled eyes to Asha. "Can you calm her?"

Asha smiled kindly and kneeled to put her hand on Theresa's chest.

After a few seconds, Theresa's sobs quieted. Tears continued to pour as she repeated *my baby* over and over.

Addison's heart was breaking. "Mom, please talk to me."

"I remember everything. You're right, you're not my child. My baby died a week after she was born. I had no one to help me with my grief. One day, I drove to the cliffs near my home and stood on the edge. I was ready to jump and join my daughter in heaven."

Addison's heart lurched. Every emotion Theresa was feeling was pouring out of her. Everyone in the room with even a hint of empathy was mourning with her.

"A woman appeared with fiery curls and blue eyes the color of the sky. She had a baby in her arms. I could tell something was wrong with the woman. She looked panicked, constantly darting her eyes around. She shoved you in my arms and told me I was your mother. Then she apologized as she laid her hand on my shoulder. My grief was wiped clean and memories of your birth and first few months flooded my mind. She compelled me to leave and move far away."

"That was my brave Addison." Addison looked up to find Marilyn holding hands with a man as they looked down at her. "We were friends with your mother. Something had happened to twist your mother's mind. She was losing touch with reality. A dangerous thing for such a powerful witch. We were watching closely to ensure your safety, but she slipped away in the night. We tracked her to the cliffs and got there as Theresa drove off with you. Without you to ground her, your mother lost her mind. She ranted about hexes, and evil coming for her. We tried to calm her, but she lashed out, putting a spell over me and changing Antony," Marilyn squeezed the man's hand, "into a cat. A part of her spell was set so we would watch over you without knowing who you were. I'm so sorry we couldn't stop her." Marilyn ended with a sob.

Theresa reached up and grabbed Asha's hand. "Please take my pain away. Lock it back up. I don't want to feel this ache anymore."

"Your daughter deserves to be remembered. I'll lessen the pain, but only you can move on from it. You'll thank me one day." She touched Theresa again and a few seconds later, the grief rolling off her that was affecting everyone was lessened to a manageable amount.

Addison helped Theresa off the floor. Marilyn wrapped them both in a hug. "Thank you for taking care of Addison all these years. Her mother would be proud."

"Wait, my mother. What happened to her after she spelled you?" Hope bloomed in Addison's chest.

Marilyn and Antony looked at each other. "We don't know. I assume the madness caused her to jump off the cliffs."

That was the logical conclusion. Without knowing for sure though, Addison wasn't going to give up all hope. Maybe her mother was still out there. She had to believe it. The alternative was too painful to bear.

five

ADDISON DIDN'T KEEP secrets from her sons. She had invited them over after she got off work. It was time to tell them about their grandmother. They were going to notice something was up anyway.

Leo sat on the loveseat, Francesca next to him. Their hands rested on the cushion between them like they were both waiting for the other to grab their hand. Francesca, being a ghost, really put a damper on all that. At this rate, she was never going to be a grandma.

Fitz and Iggy were on the big couch. Iggy was always her sensitive boy. He could tell something was off and was strangling the pillow in his lap.

It was déjà vu all over again. It wasn't that long

ago she sat them all down and told them she was divorcing their dad. This news was likely going to upset them more. They knew their marriage wasn't a happy one, so they were relieved more than anything when she told them.

Addison rolled her shoulders and blew out a breath. Time to put her big girl panties on. "Did any of you talk to Grandma yet?"

All three shook their heads. Leo managed to pull his attention away from Francesca. "I went over this morning before going to work, but she was still in bed. Now that I think about it, that is odd. She's always up early."

Leo and Fitz sat forward. They'd finally picked up on the vibe in the room.

"You guys know we found that grimoire, but what you don't know is what it said inside. It describes a powerful witch family who names every female Addison. We couldn't figure out why my name was in there, but Grandma's name isn't Addison, so we did a DNA test. It turns out she isn't my birth mother."

Francesca gasped dramatically, like she hadn't already known this.

The boys instantly talked over each other.

"That's bullshit. She's your mother and our grandmother." Fitz paced the floor.

"Maybe the test results were wrong?" Iggy offered hopefully.

Leo looked devastated. "Are you okay?"

Addison held her hand up to stop them. "There was a spell put on her by my birth mother. The why of what brought her to meet my mom is her story to tell when she is ready. This doesn't change anything between us and she is and always will be your grandmother."

"What about your birth mother?" Iggy chewed his nail as his leg bounced up and down.

"Well, we aren't sure. It turns out Marilyn was spelled as well, and she was my birth mother's friend. Either my mother threw herself off a cliff or she is out there somewhere."

"Jesus, Mom. That was bleak." Fitz shook his head at her.

"Sorry. I'm being literal, though. Marilyn saw her on the edge of a cliff in some kind of manic episode. My mother spelled her so she has no memory of what happened next."

Addison got up and walked toward the front door.

"You're leaving now?" Leo demanded.

"No. Luna is here. I was opening the door for her. She already knows everything." Addison loved her new ability to recognize people coming. Luna's normally calm energy was ragged. She opened the door and stopped short. "You don't look so good. Are you okay?"

The bags under Luna's eyes were almost purple, and her normally stylish hair was flat and tossed in a messy bun. "Actually, that's why I'm here. Can we talk?"

"Absolutely. The boys are here, but they can entertain themselves for a while." She rushed back to the living room. "I need to talk to Luna in the office. I'll be back." She spun around and then stopped. "Oh, and by the way, Marilyn's cat Cleopatra was actually her husband who was transformed as part of the spell. So yeah, no more cat. Now there's a man with a Scottish accent. You probably won't see them around for a while. They are traveling and checking with old contacts if there has been any sign of my birth mom since the day at the cliffs."

She could tell they didn't know whether to believe her or not. That's okay. It would give them something to discuss while they waited for her.

Alexander sat in the office talking to Nutmeg.

Apparently, they both had a love for poetry and had been discussing it non-stop. Addison had had enough and banished them to the office.

"Hey, Alexander. I need to talk with Luna for a minute. Do you mind excusing us?"

The ghost hopped up and bowed to Luna. "Of course."

Addison didn't bother asking Nutmeg to leave. He was in time out while her kids were over with a threat that she would put him in a dog carrier if he left the room. She was planning to tell the boys about him. Today probably wasn't the best though. She did just drop a major bomb on them.

Nutmeg turned his back to her. "Are you sure you don't want me to go? You can't hold me captive forever."

Addison rolled her eyes. "You're not captive. Stop being so dramatic. You big baby."

Luna was oblivious to their argument as she dropped down in the recliner in the corner and covered her face. "He is making my life hell." Her words were muffled under her hands.

Addison knew instantly she was talking about the man who had been in the shop yesterday. And this was serious. Luna normally wore clothing colors so bright they could blind you. Today she was in black joggers and a black t-shirt. She wanted her shiny, happy Luna back. "Who is he?"

She flopped her head back against the chair. "His name is Malachi Darkwood. He's a very powerful warlock and, for some reason, he wants my shop. He said if I don't sell to him, he'll make my life hell until I give in."

"It's not like the town has a rule we can't have similar shops. Why can't he open his own?"

Luna threw her hands in the air. "Exactly. I tried to tell him that. He said he had to have my shop."

Addison knew in her gut this was about more than the shop. What was he after, though? "Why don't we call Xavier? He can investigate the guy."

Behind her, Nutmeg made kissy sounds. "Ooh. You gonna call your boyfriend. Let's see how fast he runs over here."

Addison rolled her eyes. "You know he's not my boyfriend. Grow up."

Nutmeg held his tiny paws up. "Hey, don't get mad at me because neither of you has made a move yet." He turned to Luna. "You wouldn't believe the thoughts she has about that guy. It's X-rated, really. I'm way too innocent to see that kind of stuff."

Heat rushed to Addison's face. She chucked a couch cushion at him and missed by inches. "Seriously, I don't want the connection with you if all you're going to do is read my mind and share my inner-"

"Fantasies?" he interjected.

"Inner thoughts." She shot back.

"All I'm saying is, what you want to do with him and a watermelon-"

Addison dove at Nutmeg to stop him from finishing his sentence. The bastard was a little too fast and scurried around and into the dog cage in the corner. Addison had managed to knock over a lamp, a stack of books, and a thankfully unlit candle before skidding to a stop outside the cage.

The office door burst open. Her boys rushed in to help her. They spun left and right, trying to find the danger. All they saw was Luna in the recliner, laughing hysterically while Addison was on the floor, gasping for breath.

Leo dropped down next to her. "Are you okay? What happened?" As she was about to answer, he noticed the dog cage next to her. "Did you get a dog?"

He looked in and then moved back for his brothers to look in.

"Is that a prairie dog?" Fitz asked.

"I think it's a beaver," Leo replied.

Iggy shook his head. "No, I think it's a capybara. Why is it wearing clothes?"

Leo leaned down to look again. "Oh Mom, why are you dressing a wild animal up? What if it has rabies?"

The clothing was a good point. Somehow Nutmeg had changed outfits three times already, yet she never saw a suitcase or anything with him.

The cage door swung open. Nutmeg walked out and stood straight on his hind legs. He smiled at them. "The name's Nutmeg. Nice to meet you. And for the record, I'm a groundhog."

Leo screamed.

Iggy screamed.

Fitz screamed.

Oops. There was probably a better way to introduce him.

THE BOYS WERE FINALLY GONE. They'd asked Nutmeg a hundred questions. Some he didn't have the answer to. Like 'How were you summoned here?' and 'Could you switch to another witch if you didn't like Addison?'. It was quite rude of the vermin to actually ponder what a good idea that last one was.

She opened her front door as Xavier was raising his hand to knock. "Hi there. Thank you for coming over." She leaned in and whispered. "You're here because Luna needs your help."

Xavier's smile turned to a frown. "She needs help from a normie? I doubt that."

Addison sighed. "Please do this as a favor to me. She's really upset."

He stepped past her. "Fine. I look forward to having you owe me something in return." The way his eyes slid down her body made her shiver. He probably didn't mean it sexually, but damn it if Addison hadn't wanted him to.

He stopped and turned back. He was close enough she could see the tiny gold flecks in his green eyes. "You know, you could invite me over some time to just hang out. Or we could go out sometime?"

Awkward silence ensued. Yes, of course she wanted that. But no, she didn't want to fall in love. Could he handle a casual relationship? "How about you ask me again after we've dealt with this little crisis?"

All she wanted right now was for him to scratch a serious itch she had. Her nipples hardened at the thought.

Damn it. Even when she wasn't casting, they were popping out. She crossed her arms in front of her. "Um, should we head back?"

He glanced down at her arms and chuckled. Had he seen her turkeys were done? Did he know she was hiding them now? Why were her nipples betraying her like this?

She led him back to the office where Alexander

was reciting poetry to a very bored-looking Luna and Francesca. Nutmeg was nowhere to be seen and that worried Addison.

Xavier took the empty seat on the couch across from Luna. "I heard you have a problem."

It proved how scared Luna was when she didn't have a snarky response. "I do, and Addison seems to think you can help."

He leaned back. "Lay it on me. I promise to help if I can."

Addison was impressed. They were being such grown-ups.

"There is a warlock named Malachi Darkwood who is threatening me. He wants me to sell him my shop. If I don't, he'll take it and I'll be left with noth-ing." She took an unsteady breath. "I guess I should be thankful he's at least offering me a buyout first."

Addison leaned on the edge of her desk. "That is rather nice for an extortionist."

Xavier shrugged. "It's not really surprising. In the magical community, your reputation is every-thing. If he can get what he wants peacefully, he'll try to. It's very rare for someone to force another magic user to do something. That must mean there is something about your shop he wants bad."

That didn't make Addison feel any better. "Do

you think you can look into him and see if you can figure out what he wants?"

Xavier glanced over and saw the dog carrier. He answered as he stared at the crate. "I'm sure he's going to keep his reasoning very close to his vest. I'll see what I can find out, though. If nothing else, maybe I can find some ammunition you can use against him. If he wants to be an extortionist, you can be a blackmailer."

He got up from the couch and crouched in front of the cage. "What do you have in there?"

The cage door popped open. Nutmeg strutted out. "Xavier, nice to finally meet you."

Addison gave the man credit. He didn't scream. He did fall backward onto his butt and scurry back a few paces. "Why do you have a talking gopher?"

Addison bit her cheek to keep from laughing. The big, bad paranormal investigator is afraid of Nutmeg?

"This is the guy, really?" Nutmeg hopped up on the coffee table so he was face to face with Xavier who was still on the ground. "You've never seen a familiar before?"

Xavier cleared his throat as he got up. He took the time to brush off his impeccable suit before answering. "Of course, I know about familiars. You caught me off guard. Last I saw Addison, she didn't have one. They also usually don't talk, and I've never seen one wear clothes."

Addison's eyebrows drew together. "Is that true?"

Nutmeg smiled proudly. "To your first point. You are correct that familiars don't talk to anyone except their partner. The Schmidt line is very old so I'm a bit more juiced up than your regular familiar. On your second point, yeah, what's up with them not wearing clothes? I mean, I want to look good." He waved his paw up and down his body and then pointed at Xavier. "You understand, you're a man of class, like Alexander, too."

Great, she had the only familiar in the world with a taste for fashion. Was he going to expect her to buy him clothes? Where did she even get something that small? A doll store maybe? He'd fit in preemie clothes, but he probably wouldn't like being put in a onesie.

"Oh my god, Nutmeg, no."

Luna's screech snapped Addison out of her thoughts. "What did I miss?"

Luna had her hand across the furball's face. "He was telling Xavier that he knew all about him because of the connection with you and started to tell him what he'd seen in your head."

Addison glared at the familiar. "You know, we haven't done the spell to fully connect us. I'm happy to send you packing."

Like a true gentleman, Xavier didn't acknowledge the implication Nutmeg was trying to make. "You don't want to send him away. A familiar can help keep you safe. They amplify your magic an insane amount. And there's a rumor that the place where rejected familiars go isn't a very good one."

All eyes snapped to Nutmeg. Luna pulled her hand away and sat back in the recliner. "Is that true?"

Nutmeg crossed his paws. "That is familiar business."

Through the faint connection Addison did have with him, she could feel his fear. No matter how much he drove her crazy, she would never send him away.

He must have read her mind. He glanced up at her, smiled, and gave her a tiny nod.

Xavier cleared his throat. "Well, back to business at hand. If Malachi wants your shop bad enough to risk his reputation, then he probably shouldn't have it. I'll look into him. You guys should go to the shop and set up as many wards as you can. If he's as powerful as you say he is, they may not help, but it's better to be safe than sorry. Nutmeg should probably keep a low profile in public until you master shielding him. The dog carrier is probably a good idea."

Addison had a feeling that idea was going to go over like a lead balloon. Why couldn't she have a sweet, easygoing familiar?

seven

ADDISON PLOPPED into the chair in Luna's shop and dropped the dog carrier on the table. "I could have left you home, you know."

"I didn't know you were going to lock the door of this thing. Come on, let me out. This is not cool," Nutmeg pleaded from behind the tiny metal door.

She did feel a little bad. "It's just for appearances, okay? When humans aren't around, you can roam free."

Addison took a deep breath. *The Soul Apothecary* was quickly becoming one of her favorite places. There was always an undercurrent of magic humming around them.

The bell over the door rang as Addison sensed Minnie coming in. "Oh good, you're here."

Minnie gave her a droll look. "Of course. You said you needed my help. The coven has promised me up on a shiny platter to be at your beck and call."

Addison had learned quickly to ignore the snark and act like everything Minnie said was from a place of warmth and friendship. "And we appreciate your sacrifice. Now, for the issue at hand. There is a warlock named Malachi Darkwood who is trying to take Luna's shop by force. Since you are such an amazing and powerful witch, I was hoping your magic would be exactly what we needed to keep him out."

She'd also learned flattery got you far with her emotional support witch.

Minnie snorted. "Well, you're not wrong there. Are we all set?"

Luna walked in from the back room. Her arms were full of items, including a jar of those gross eyeballs Addison hated looking at. "I think I have everything we need. If you see something I'm missing, let me know."

Minnie and Luna went through the pile and talked back and forth over the benefits of each item. Addison pulled out her phone and recorded them. Minnie noticed and raised one eyebrow. "It's easier than taking notes and this way I won't forget every-thing you guys said."

Minnie nodded and went back to sorting through the items. "I don't see any mugwort. If you have wormwood, we can use that in its place."

Luna grabbed two jars off a nearby shelf and set them on the table. "I'm out of Woodruff too, but I have Deerstongue that can be used in its place."

Minnie pursed her lips as she studied the ingre-dients they'd laid out. "Excellent. It would be better if we had a drop of his blood or one of his hairs, but this will make do."

"If he comes in again, I'd be happy to stab him or yank his hair," Luna grumbled.

Addison patted her shoulder. "Now, now. Chief Novak may have moved in across the street, but that doesn't mean we're close enough that he can get you out of assault charges."

"And boy, do you want to get close to him?" Nutmeg looked all innocent as he revealed yet another one of her internal thoughts.

Minnie gasped and sat down. "Oh, do tell."

"Not if you're smart," Addison warned Nutmeg.

"You're no fun." He pouted at her.

Minnie sighed dramatically. "Yeah, spoilsport."

"All I'm saying is we drove by earlier when he

had someone pulled over. He stopped what he was doing to wave at her. You should have seen her blush. I'll spare you what she was thinking."

Addison glared at him. If looks could kill, Nutmeg would be dead ten times over.

"Can we get on with protecting my shop, please?" The bags under Luna's eyes made it clear how much the Malachi drama was affecting her. She pushed a mortar and pestle at Addison, along with a bowl of eggs. I need you to ground the eggshells into dust. Minnie, can you make a mojo spell bag while I do a candle spell?"

Addison was fascinated. This was the first time she had seen someone do in-depth potion work. Up until now, it had all been spoken spells. "Why eggshells?"

"Eggshells protect baby birds from outside threats. We include it to help ward off malicious intent." Luna answered as she mixed several herbs into a bowl. "I'm combining cinnamon, peppermint, rosemary, and Sacred Lotus to protect me from energies, spirits, and people with harmful intentions."

Once the mixture was combined, she added in the crushed eggshell. She grabbed a small candle, rolled it in the mixture until it was covered, and then set it on a small glass dish.

The lights dimmed magically as she lit the flame and recited each ingredient and the intention she wanted from it.

Luna stayed silent as she watched the candle burn. Minnie was still filling a small velvet pouch with ingredients. Uncharacteristically, both she and Nutmeg were silent, so she followed suit.

When the flame finally went out, the store lights returned. For the first time in two days, Luna had a genuine smile on her face. "Between this stuff and the wards I boosted last night, I feel much better about Malachi's chances of bothering the store."

"I was good during your ritual. Can I come out now?" Nutmeg pleaded.

Addison squinted at him. "Fine, but don't cause any trouble." She opened the door and chuckled as he strutted out.

They walked around, putting everything back in its place while Nutmeg lounged on a shelf with glass orbs on them. He stared into one. On the other side, his face was distorted and large. He looked ridiculous. Addison didn't say anything though. It felt like he was actually seeing or communicating with something and she wasn't going to mess with anything she didn't understand.

She passed a new display of necklaces. "Why are there nails as necklace pendants?"

Luna walked up and ran her fingers through them. "It took me a while to get these in. They have to be iron and from the coffin of an occupied grave so you can imagine how hard they are to get. People wear them for protection."

The bell over the door chimed as Addison's least favorite person in the world, Augie Stilt, and her friend from the other day, entered the shop.

"Psst." Addison tried to quietly get Nutmeg's attention. It took him a minute before he looked away from the orb and noticed humans had entered.

She'd give him credit. He tried his best to get back to the carrier without being noticed. Augie was too observant for that.

"Oh my god, rodent." She screeched as she lifted her umbrella and took off after Nutmeg. She chased him up and down several aisles before Minnie was able to temporarily make him look like a cat.

When Augie finally saw it was a cat and not a rodent, she skidded to a stop. "I am so sorry. I thought it was a giant rat or something. Why is your cat in clothes, though?"

Minnie pointed at Addison. "Don't ask me. He belongs to her."

Augie looked down her nose at Addison. "Hhmmpf. I should have known."

Obnoxious lady says what?

Addison opened her mouth to cut her down as Luna stepped in front of her and handed her Nutmeg. "Why don't you take your cat in the back?"

Addison scowled at Augie before turning her back on her and stomping through the employee's only door. That woman was lucky Addison hadn't really learned magic yet or she might have to hex her. That was probably frowned upon, but come on, the woman deserved it.

eight

"I'M BORED." Nutmeg stalked back and forth in the employee area of Luna's shop. Minnie's spell had worn off, and he was back to looking like a groundhog.

Addison peeked out the door into the store. "Me too. Luna is doing her darndest, but those women won't leave."

"Can we go out back and get some fresh air? The incense in here is enough to choke a cat."

"Kind of funny, since you were just one a few minutes ago." She did agree with him, though. It was one of her least favorite parts of the shop. Did that make her a bad witch if she didn't like them? Was it an unspoken rule that all witches were supposed to like incense? That would be a question for Luna another day. No way she would ask Minnie. That woman would find a way to insult her while sounding so sweet.

She spotted a leash hanging on a hook by the back door. "We can go out, but the crate is out there. You're going to have to be on a leash and act like a pet." People already thought she was crazy. What was one more piece of gossip?

Nutmeg crossed his paws. "You are kidding, right?"

Addison tried to look apologetic, but on the inside, she was enjoying this way too much. "Sorry. I don't know how to make you look like a cat or a dog. Maybe with the leash, people will assume you're a pet and leave us alone."

"Fine. No yanking on it though!" He pouted while she put it on him. "And why does she even have a leash here?"

"Good point. It is a magic shop, so maybe we shouldn't question it?" So far, every witch and warlock she'd met seemed to be quirky and eccentric to a degree. It kind of made her love them more.

Addison expected a few odd looks as they walked down the street. It had been too much to hope for rain, so fewer people would be out. What she didn't expect was for people to outright gawk and point at her. There was no going back now. She was cementing her crazy lady status. She was fine with that as long as it didn't impact her dating life. Eight dates with eight different men so far and she loved the freedom to have a good time and then walk away with no strings attached. Only one had pushed hard for a second date. It was very obvious he was looking for something more serious than she was ready to give.

Nutmeg pulled on the leash as he stepped off the sidewalk. "I see a park. Let's go there."

A dog off leash ran up and tried to sniff Nutmeg's butt. He kicked out at the beagle. "Keep it moving pal."

Two women with strollers stopped and stared wide-eyed at him. "Did that creature just talk?" One of the women was truly curious, while the other looked horrified.

"It's not possible, right?"

Addison chuckled nervously. "Sorry, I had my phone call on speaker. It sounded like my pet talked, didn't it? Weird."

She left them with confused looks and rushed into the park. "Dude. You can't talk in front of the humans."

He had the sense to look sorry. "My bad. Most of

your family isolated themselves from the human world. I'm not used to having to blend in."

Addison gasped. She steered him behind a line of trees so they were out of sight. "That's right, you said before you're connected to my family. It didn't register until right now. Did you know my mother?" She held her breath as she waited for his answer.

"I met her a couple of times. I hadn't seen her in a very long time, well before she was even pregnant with you. I was with your great aunt Addison."

"Doesn't that get confusing at family gatherings, having every female with the same name?" She tried to picture passing out Christmas presents when every tag said - to Addison, from Addison.

"There's never more than a couple alive at the same time. The rare times they are together, they use nicknames. The oldest is called Addison while the others go by Ads or Addie. There was a cousin once who wanted to be called Dison. She was an odd one. And that's saying something when you're talking about a witch from an old magick family."

"What did my mom look like?" Addison felt like a child asking, but she was too curious not to.

He smiled up at her. "You are the spitting image of her. I mean, all the Addison's look extremely simi-lar. You though, look like a clone of her."

Warmth filled her. Just thinking she looked like her mom gave her some peace. It also made her feel guilty because the mom she already had was pretty amazing. She had so many conflicting feelings.

"Wow, you feel that?" Nutmeg's hair was standing up.

Addison focused on her surroundings and felt a strong power radiating from behind a cluster of trees and bushes. Being the act first and ask questions later type she immediately went to it. There was a slight hum that grew louder as they got near. She stepped aside a large bush and skidded to a stop. "What on Earth?"

"That's just it. I don't think that is on Earth." Nutmeg studied the swirling void of smoke.

Addison was lost. "What does that mean?"

"I've seen these before. It's a portal to another dimension." He picked up a small rock and tossed it in.

Addison leaned close to brush her hand over the top of it. Cold radiated from the smoke. She screeched and windmilled her arms as her flip-flop slid on the edge of the void. She felt a thump against her chest that sent her careening backward to safety. As she was falling, she saw Nutmeg heading right toward the void. He'd jumped at her to knock her back, and the force sent him flying right at the portal.

She remembered the leash and yanked with all her might. He snapped back and landed right in her lap. Addison's heart was thumping in her chest. "Holy crap. You saved me and I saved you. That was seriously scary."

Nutmeg looked up at her with big watery eyes. "I really thought you didn't like me. You could have let me go and no one would have known."

Addison's jaw dropped. "Oh my god, I would never have done that! You can see in my head. Sure, I'm having a lot of confusing thoughts, but I don't hate you. If anything, I don't want to let you out of my sight. You can tell me so much about my family. And from what you've told me, you are my family, too."

Her heart melted as he snuggled his face against her and did his best to hug her with his tiny arms.

She gave him a few seconds, then scooped him in her arms and stood up. "Come on. Let's cover this up and tell the others about it."

Nutmeg jumped down and went right to work. Maybe they had turned a page in their new relationship. Goodness knows she could use one less person in her life full of snark.

nine

ADDISON WAS COCOONED in her blanket, trying desperately to fall asleep. So far, it was mostly watching the fan spin. She'd tried counting sheep, and even groundhogs, but nothing worked. She couldn't stop thinking about the portal.

She'd texted the Schmidties, the name she labeled the group chat in her phone that included Luna, Minnie, and Xavier, and told them all about it. They agreed they would go tomorrow after Addison got off work.

How could they wait though? Another dimension? That's like once in a lifetime kind of thing. She assumed, at least. She was new to all of this, so what did she really know?

When the clock read two a.m. she was done with

laying there. Nutmeg was sound asleep in the guest room. He insisted on having a full-sized bed all to himself. For now, she would give in to his demands. At least until she needed the room for a real guest.

She dressed quietly and made sure to wear her boots that had a good tread. If she was going into that portal, it would be on her terms. Not because she fell in. She packed a bag with water, granola bars, a first-aid kit, and the crystals she'd bought from Luna. Who knew what you'd need in another realm?

On her way to her car, Chief Novak pulled into Cecil's driveway across the street. Theo had moved in with his grandfather when it became clear it was too dangerous to let the older man live on his own.

Addison had been over to visit Cecil a few times to ask about his revelation that he knew about the paranormal world. Unfortunately, every time she brought it up, he looked at her like she was insane. The dementia was too hard to break through and she hadn't managed to catch him on a lucid day yet.

She waved at Theo, hoping he'd wave and go inside. No such luck. He grabbed a duffle bag out of the back of his police SUV and crossed the street. "I know the coffee shop opens early, but this is ridiculous."

She loved the soft lilt of his voice. "No work for me. I couldn't sleep so I'm going for a drive. It's too crowded in my house."

He leaned to look around her. "Don't you live alone?"

Crap. He didn't know about the ghosts and the talking groundhog. "Yeah. I do. I meant the walls were crowding me in. I like the open air when I have insomnia."

He nodded as he contemplated her words. "Gotcha. This probably seems an odd time to ask, but I was wondering if you wanted to go out sometime? We could get a drink or dinner."

Addison's jaw dropped open. She shut it quickly. "You mean like me, you, and Cecil?"

He gave her a panting-dropping smirk. "Nope. Just you and me."

"Ha!" She hadn't meant to say that so loud. "Sorry. That sounds amazing, but you are like way younger than me. I am deeply, deeply flattered. I don't think I could do it, though. I'd feel like I was out with one of my sons."

He stepped closer to her. "I know I'm older than your sons and not that much younger than you. Even if I was, who cares? I'm the Chief of Police. That has to buy me some leeway from the gossips, right?"

He was making it very hard to say no. Living across the street from her though, would be the exact opposite of a no strings attached fling. There would be strings, and they would probably feel amazing. That was not what she wanted, though. "It's a tempting offer. I'm not comfortable with the idea, though."

He studied her for a second before blowing out a breath. "I understand. If you change your mind, I'm only 30 yards away and you have my personal cell number. Use it sometime." He winked and left.

She didn't move as she watched him cross the street and go inside. Luna was going to die when she told her about this.

When he was out of sight, she turned back to her car. For a few seconds, she couldn't remember why she was out there.

Right, the portal to another realm. There was no way she'd be able to sleep now after that proposition from Theo. She might as well burn off some of the nervous energy thrumming through her body.

At the entrance to the park, she had a moment of hesitation. She'd never really been a huge fan of the dark. Shit hides in the dark. And the park was pitch black since it was closed. She stared at herself in the rearview mirror. "Come on. You are a forty-six-year-old woman. Get your ass out of the car."

Properly chastised, she took a deep breath, grabbed her backpack of supplies, and went inside.

Every rustle of a leaf or snap of a twig had Addison spinning around and shining her phone's flashlight. One of the first things she wanted to do was learn defensive magic. She wanted to walk in the dark and know she could handle anything that came at her.

Now that she'd been close to the portal, she was able to recognize the hum of power before she was even close.

She carefully pulled the branches away that she and Nutmeg had used to cover the portal. The inky swirl made her shudder. How could it be so scary yet so exciting at the same time?

Her hand shook as she reached out to graze the top of the mist. Every horror movie she'd ever seen prepared her for something to reach out of the hole and pull her in.

She shrieked when someone coughed. She landed backward on her ass. Her heart was pounding. She hopped up as fast as she could and spun around, shining her flashlight in every direction.

Nothing. She'd heard someone. Animals didn't cough like that.

"Okay. You've had your fun. Nutmeg or Minnie, you can come out now." They must have known not to trust that she would wait until the next day.

When no one came out, a shiver of fear ran down her spine. "Maybe I should come back in the daylight. There's no reason I can't wait. Safety in numbers, after all."

She bent over to drag the branches back over the portal when she heard it again. A tiny cough.

"Okay. Seriously, not funny. Come on, guys." At that moment, she was glad her magic was chaotic. They deserved whatever she was going to do to them.

"Excuse me. I didn't mean to scare you." The soft feminine voice sounded like a young girl.

Why would a child be out at this hour? "It's okay. I won't hurt you. If you need help, I can get you back to your family."

The voice giggled. "Look down." Addison pointed her flashlight toward the ground and saw a tiny movement on a rock by her foot. "Evening. Or I guess morning. You might want to avoid that portal if you don't want to die."

Crazy fairy says what?

Addison sat on the ground to get closer. "You know where it leads?"

The brunette with rosy cheeks and iridescent wings turned solemn as she nodded. "That takes you to a realm controlled by dark forces. You probably don't want to go in there."

That may be true, but the portal was calling to her. It was why she wasn't able to sleep and was creeping around a dark park in the middle of the night. "Have you been there?"

"I have, and I will be going back. I'm going to need help, though. There is a bad man there I need to defeat. I don't think I can do it on my own, though." She cocked her head and studied Addison. "You have some serious magical juice in you. Want to team up? I could guide you. You'd have to sign this contract, though."

A rolled-up piece of parchment appeared floating in front of Addison, along with a feather quill pen.

This night couldn't get much weirder. Addison unrolled the contract and scanned through it. The gist was that the fae was not responsible for any injury, death, or dismemberment she could incur while being guided. There would be no favors owed, and everyone would be free to go their own way when the mission was completed.

"This is pretty intense. Do you have a lot of death and dismemberment when you guide people?" She had been joking, but stopped laughing when the fae shrugged.

"It happens. It is a dark realm, after all. My success rate is one of the highest in my clan. And if you ever run into Simon, don't listen to anything he has to say. I warned him not to stick his arm in that hole. He did anyway and now he's one appendage short. That was on him for not listening." She crossed her arms petulantly. She looked a little ridiculous with her red t-shirt, black pants, and combat boots. Where did she even get clothes that tiny? They totally didn't match with her gentle fae features.

She wasn't making Addison feel better about being her guide. "So, who is the man you are trying to defeat? What did he do?"

"His name is Malachi. He's been trying to open a bridge between that dark realm and the fae realm."

"Wait, Malachi Darkwood?" What were the odds?

The fae flitted up and down. "Yes, do you know of him?"

Addison blew out a breath. "You could say that. He's threatening my friend. She was such joy and light until he came along. It's like he's drained all the goodness out of her."

The fae reached out her tiny hand and patted Addison's knee. "I understand completely. You could save her, though. Help me take him down and she'll be free of him. We all will."

Addison was so torn. It would be nice to get rid of Luna's problems. And from what Addison had read, the fae were extremely powerful in their own right. Would the two of them alone be enough to stop Malachi, though?

The fae snorted. "I can practically see the wheels turning in your head. No, my kind doesn't get bigger like some other kinds do. That doesn't mean my magic is any weaker." As a demonstration, she snapped her fingers, and the ground grew underneath Addison and formed a chair. A branch from a nearby tree used its leaves to brush her off as several birds, bunnies, and squirrels came into the area and surrounded her. She could sense they had no malice toward her. She bent down and petted one of the bunnies who turned its head and let her scratch its ear.

Addison held her breath as she grabbed the pen

and signed the contract. Before the ink was even dry, the parchment disappeared.

The fae smiled proudly. "If you're satisfied, we can get a move on. My name's Clarice and we need to go over the do's and don'ts, so we keep you in one piece."

Clarice really needed to work on her delivery. For every sentence that made Addison feel better about their plan, she'd say another and destroy any confidence Addison had about her.

She stared down at the swirling abyss. "Screw it. Let's do this for Luna."

ten

"YOU HAVE TO UNDERSTAND, there are a lot of things in the dark realm that want to kill you. Most of them are monsters with no logical thought. They smell a stranger and they hunt you."

Addison was truly regretting that she had signed the contract with Clarice. She was way in over her head.

Clarice waved her hand and a new piece of parchment floated in front of Addison's face. "These are just a few things you should and shouldn't do. You'd do well to memorize them."

- Never stop to smell the flowers. They will release poisonous gas.

- Never offer to help anything that may ask for it. It's likely a trap.
- Never ask for directions. It's definitely a trap.
- Never drink from any standing water, lakes, or ponds.
- When it's a blood moon, you may drink the rain as it falls from the sky. This is the only time it is water. Don't ask what it is the rest of the time. You don't want to know.
- Never follow a sign as directed. If it says go left, you go right, etc.
- Never trust your senses. What you smell is not what it is. What you see is likely not there.
- Never believe the lies that are whispered from the mist.
- Always do the opposite of what your gut is telling you. The intuition you feel isn't your own.
- Always be watching your front and your back at the same time.

WHAT.THE.HELL.

Addison looked around the paper to glare at the fairy. "How in the hell do I navigate this place? I literally can't watch my front and my back at the same time. Why would anyone go in this place?"

"You are in big trouble, young lady." Addison and Clarice jumped at the voice coming from the bushes. People really needed to stop doing that.

Nutmeg walked into the clearing a second later. "I had to be woken up by Alexander and Francesca telling me you took off. They noticed you put on sneakers instead of your usual flip-flops and knew you were up to something. I knew exactly where you were headed. I told Minnie you wouldn't be able to wait. What were you thinking coming here alone?"

Addison felt like a child being chastised by her father. Then she remembered she was a grown-ass adult. "I don't need your permission to leave my house or to go into a portal to a dark realm where everything wants to kill me and I'll probably lose an arm."

He cocked his head. "What are you talking about?"

Clarice flew up from the rock and got his attention. "Hello. I'm Clarice and I'm going to be her guide as we travel the dark realm and hunt Malachi Darkwood. She signed a contract and everything."

Nutmeg slowly dragged his eyes back to Addison. "I don't know who is going to be more pissed, Luna, Minnie, or Xavier. You are in so much trouble."

Addison's stomach did a little flop. She didn't want any of her new friends mad at her. "If I can stop Malachi, they'll forget all about being mad at me and Luna will be so relieved her problem is resolved."

The grumpy groundhog climbed up on her lap and glared at her. "We are stronger together. Not just you and me, your friends too."

"Well, now that you're here, I'm sure everything will be fine." She really would feel better if he was by her side. She didn't trust Clarice. Nutmeg though, would never leave her.

Clarice cleared her throat. "He can't go in without signing a contract." The parchment and quill pen appeared in front of him.

He held up his paw. "How exactly do you expect me to do that?"

The fairy tapped her chin in contemplation. "I'm not sure. I can't guide you without a signature. It's my job."

Nutmeg glanced back at Addison. "She doesn't own the portal. We can go in without her."

Clarice gasped. Her face reddened in anger.

Addison shook her head. "She's been inside before. I'd rather go with someone who knows what to expect. It's going to be fine."

He grumbled as he climbed down and stuck his paw into some mud and walked back to the contract. He left his paw print on the signature line. "Fine. We good?"

Clarice went back into her thinking pose for a few seconds. "I think this will be acceptable. Are we ready to go?"

Addison held her hand up. "Not yet. He needs to read the list showing what we should and shouldn't do."

The paper appeared in front of his face. He was silent as he read through it. When he finished, his rounded eyes swung around to Addison. "You are an idiot. You probably had us sign our death certificate. How do you expect to deal with all this?"

Addison couldn't hide the unease she felt. "I don't know. I know I have the best familiar in all the realms, though. Together, we can do this." Maybe flattery would appease him.

"I'm not falling for that. There has to be a better way to do this."

Clarice giggled. "Of course there is. I can give you this potion and it will negate almost everything on that list for two hours."

Addison and Nutmeg's jaws fell open.

Addison threw her hands in the air. "Why didn't you offer that to begin with?"

The tiny fairy shrugged. "You didn't ask. I gave you our standard spiel."

Addison closed her eyes and counted to ten. Why were fairies so popular with humans? They were serious pains in the asses. "Fine. Give us the potion and let's get this over with."

A small bottle appeared in Addison's hand. An even tinier bottle appeared in Nutmeg's paw. She had a moment of hesitation before pulling the cork out and downing the liquid. It tasted like a strawberry daiquiri. At least there was one positive in all this.

Goosebumps ran across her skin as she felt an iciness flow through her veins. Nutmeg's hair stood on end as his eyes glowed neon green for a second. Had her eyes done that?

Clarice flew onto Addison's shoulder as she

grabbed Nutmeg and stood up. "Okay, what do we do?"

"Walk into it silly." Clarice laughed like it was the silliest thing Addison could have said.

"It looks like a hole. Am I going to fall through and hurtle through the air on the other side?"

"You have the craziest ideas. You'll step in and step out on the other side."

"Don't question it anymore. Portals make no sense to anyone except the fae," Nutmeg said from his spot tucked under her arm.

"Okay. Here goes nothing." She held her breath and stepped in.

eleven

ADDISON'S FOOT landed with a thud. All laws of physics demanded she be hurtling through the air right now, but it was like the world turned on its side with her and she walked right out like she'd stepped through a door. Weird.

They stood in the woods, a thick mist surrounding them. It was twilight and sweltering. "I can imagine why Malachi wants to get into your realm. It has to be nicer than this place."

"It wasn't always like this. The more evil that settled here, the more poisoned the realm became. The sun never rises. It really messes with your sense of time, but so does everything else about this place."

Addison wanted to question how trees and

flowers grew without the sun. She already knew that answer though, magic.

A howl in the distance had her spinning around. Nutmeg cursed at the same time she did. The portal was gone. Clarice hadn't warned them about that. Before she could question how they were getting home, loud whispers echoed all around them. Footsteps thundered on the ground as something ran toward them.

She, for one, didn't want to find out what it was. "Where do I go?"

"The opposite way of those footsteps is a good start." Nutmeg wasn't very helpful.

"What about the mist? I feel like it's so thick I'll need to cut through it." She wasn't exaggerating. It looked like a solid wall encircling her.

"Just go. It'll be fine." Clarice squealed.

Addison wasn't feeling very good about her guide being scared, too. "Here goes nothing." She ran straight at the mist hoping it wasn't as solid as it looked.

Amazingly, as she ran, the mist moved around her. She always had a clear bubble three feet in every direction. That was nice of the creepy fog to not completely blind her.

They were heading toward a fork in the road.

One sign said Earth and one said Fae. Without thinking, she turned down the path toward Earth.

Clarice screeched as Addison remembered she wasn't supposed to follow signs. The ground disappeared under her feet as she slid down an embankment. Rocks dug into her skin as she fell. She imagined a shelf and tried using her magic, hoping that would stop her. Nothing happened. Of course not. She hasn't had any training yet. Why did she think she could do this?

She slid for so long she was starting to worry it was a never-ending slope when she finally hit the ground with a thud. Nutmeg had crawled inside her shirt during the drama, so he reappeared unscathed. "We should probably have a conversation about personal space."

He huffed at her. "That was no picnic for me either. It was that or get as cut up as you are. Don't worry, I kept my eyes closed. I didn't see your neon pink bra."

She gasped. "Aha. You did or you wouldn't know what color it is." He had a point though. "But if you need to hide in there again, you can, with your eyes closed."

Clarice flew down and landed on Addison's shoulder. "I tried to catch you guys, but you were so dang fast and the mist bubble followed you, so I was blinded. I had to follow your screams to find you again."

Addison brushed the dirt and gravel off her ripped clothes. "We're off to a great start. Do you know how to find Malachi? You are supposed to be guiding us, right?"

Clarice twisted her hands nervously in front of her.

"I have a feeling Clarice wasn't very forthcoming about her skill set." Nutmeg whispered.

Addison prayed he was wrong. She wouldn't have agreed to bring them here if she didn't know what she was doing, right?

Clarice bit her nail. "Well, here's the thing, I don't actually know how to find him." Addison's eyes widened as she opened her mouth to yell at the fairy when the little pain in the ass held her hands up. "I'm sure together we can find him. You two are the most powerful witch/familiar combo I've come across in a long time. You should be able to take care of anything we run into."

It was Addison's turn to look uncomfortable. "I've only known about magic for a month. My powers had been blocked my entire life. I don't know how to do anything purposeful with it. Stick with me and I'm sure I'll set something on fire or enlarge something accidentally."

Clarice audibly gulped. "This is quite the conundrum. No matter, we're here now. We might as well keep going."

Nutmeg snorted. "I don't know which of you is worse."

Addison was going to get so much shit from the Schmidties when she got back. "Okay. My gut is telling me to head toward that mountain over there. Your rules said to do the opposite, so I guess we head the opposite way."

They made their way through the forest. Flowers in every shape and color bloomed in the darkness. They were gorgeous. Marilyn would be going crazy. Maybe she should bring some back for her.

She reached her hand out and Nutmeg yanked her hair. "If the rules said we can't smell the flowers, I think we should steer clear of them, don't you?"

Damn rules.

They walked for what felt like forever. Her bottle of water was nearly empty. The heat and humidity were worse than Florida in the dead of summer. Worst of all, the potion had to be wearing off. The voices in the mist were talking much more clearly and a whole lot louder. They were mean and nasty throwing out insults about her, her clothes, and even a few about Nutmeg. It wasn't until they started getting more personal, telling her how unloved she was that it got harder to ignore them.

The air around them turned frigid as something stalked them through the trees. Before they could decide which way to go, they were surrounded by foul-smelling yeti-like creatures. The biggest difference between these monsters and the ones on Earth was the large horns protruding from their heads and the fact that they had two sets of arms. That had taken her a second to accept what she was seeing.

The closest creature swiped its long arm toward her. She darted away, right into the reach of another monster. Its swipe to her shoulder sent her flying off her feet. She landed four feet away.

Clarice growled, and a glow appeared around her. "You guys run. I'll stop these things and catch up to you."

As much as she hurt and was scared, Addison didn't want to leave the fairy on her own. "There's five of them. There's no way you can take them all on."

Clarice let out a roar as she sent sparks flying from her hands. The hair of the two closest creatures caught on fire. The ground around the other three shook violently as it grew up around them, trapping them. "This won't stop them for long. Keep going."

"Addison, she'll be fine. Let's go." The confidence in Nutmeg's voice was the only reason she finally agreed. This was a serious shit show.

twelve

ADDISON TOOK off through the mist. Any time her gut told her to go one way, she made sure to go the other way. At one point, she'd heard someone calling out for help and wanted to go to them. Nutmeg reminded her the rules said it would be a trap. Every bone in her body wanted her to help the voice. It felt almost shameful to walk away.

The air around them suddenly cleared, and the voices in the mist stopped as they entered an open area. A large house sat on a cliff overlooking the forest below. The peeling paint and broken window shutters made it look like it was sagging and depressed.

Magic tingled along Addison's skin. Someone had a spell over the area that worked like Clarice's potion had. She hadn't realized how miserable the realm had made her feel until the spell cleared everything away.

"I feel so much better. We're hiding here until Clarice catches up."

Nutmeg was smart enough not to argue with her. It wasn't like he had much choice. His tiny legs were never going to outrun the creatures hunting them. His best bet was to hang on to her and hope she got them out.

The smell of rotting meat tickled her nose as they got close to one of the windows of the house. She peeked in and gasped. Animals and monsters of all kinds were in cages. Some were dead and the cause of the rotten smell. The others were in various states of pain. Whoever lived there had been doing terrible things to these animals. Even if they tried to kill her in the woods, they didn't deserve this.

"Open your senses. You can feel the magic is dark, can't you? You need to learn to recognize it so you're never caught unaware."

Addison did as Nutmeg instructed and focused on the magic. At first, it felt like she was looking at a channel with static playing. "Engage your magic. You can feel where it is deep inside you. Ask it to help you."

She nodded and tried again. She pictured her magic as a glowing purple orb in her core. She asked it to help her see clearer. Almost immediately, the static went away.

The haze of the magic was different than she was used to seeing. Except for the time at the warehouse when they were searching for Antony. Now that she understood what she was looking at, it was obvious it was evil. The best way to describe it was the air tasted slightly sour and felt thicker.

Movement across the room had her falling to the ground and hiding. She couldn't believe her luck or bad luck, depending on how you looked at it. Malachi Darkwood was inside. He looked more ragged than he had the time she saw him in Luna's shop. She hadn't even noticed him sitting at a desk looking at a book until he stood up. His back had been to her, so she wasn't worried he'd seen her. "I'm going to hold you up. Peek inside and let me know if he's still there."

"What? Why me?" Nutmeg did not like her plan.

"You're smaller and so easier to hide. Plus, he'd think less of an animal looking in than a person." It sucked, but he knew she was right.

"Fine. If I end up in one of those cages, I will haunt you for the rest of your days." He scowled as she slowly lifted him so his head barely peeked over the windowsill. "He's grabbing stuff off shelves. He just picked his nose. Guess he doesn't realize we're watching him. Now he's walked out of the room."

A second later, they heard an exterior door open and shut. Addison crawled to the corner and looked around. Malachi had a bag and a book with him as he walked around the far side of the house.

She slowly crept around and followed him as he walked down a small footpath leading to the bottom of the cliff. He disappeared inside a cave. She hid behind a bush to make sure he was staying inside and not coming back out.

When he hadn't, she snuck over to the entrance and walked in. The air smelled of damp soil and incense. Small torches set every few feet, showing a long tunnel stretched in front of them. "What could go wrong?"

Nutmeg opened his mouth. She covered it with her hand. "That was rhetorical. I don't need a list."

They walked in silence. She strained to hear every little sound. If Malachi walked toward them, they'd be screwed. There was nowhere to hide. A cold sweat and nerves had her shaking.

The ground sloped downward as they went deeper. Eventually, the tunnel opened to an enormous cavern. Cabinets and tables were spread around and several doors were built into the walls. It was a maze of disorder, which was great for them. It gave them plenty of hiding places and ways to move around without being seen.

Malachi stood at an altar setting out ingredients he'd brought with him. A large book lay open in front of him.

Addison snuck behind a large armoire and glanced around it. Malachi was reciting something from the book. His hair floated around him. That must be his physical reaction, like when her nipples harden. Lucky for him.

Electricity crackled through the air. She yipped as a little bolt of energy shocked her.

Malachi froze and spun around, slowly studying the room. He took a few steps in the direction she was hiding. How in the hell was she going to get out of this one?

"Pssst. Come here."

"I don't care who that is. Follow that voice," Nutmeg demanded with an edge to his voice.

She had to hope they weren't jumping from the frying pan and into the fire.

thirteen

A FEMININE HAND stuck out from the door behind them. Addison was dirty, cut up, hungry, and tired of running for her life. Whoever was behind that door had to be better than Malachi. Addison took a split second to sense the aura of the person. She didn't think the person was malicious, so she had no choice but to go for it.

She slipped through the door seconds before Malachi rounded the armoire where they'd been hiding. They stood in silence until they heard him walk away.

The hallway was dark except for a small ball of light the woman had hovering in front of her. Addison followed her a good distance and entered another small room.

The woman used magic to light several candles in the room. Her curly red hair was standing in every direction. Her patchwork skirt and oversized sweater made Addison think of a traveling gypsy. She smiled at them. "I'm Ruella and you are far from home."

"I'm Addison and this is Nutmeg. I don't feel darkness coming from you. Do you live here?"

Ruella shook her head. "I have a feeling we're here for the same reason. Malachi destroyed my family home to obtain some artifacts we'd collected. I'm here to kill him."

Addison's eyes widened. "Our plans were loose, but I don't think killing him was a part of it."

Nutmeg snorted. "What did you think was going to happen?"

Now that he said it, it made sense. She was new to this whole hunting dark wizard thing. Killing a person wasn't really a normal thought she had. "I don't know. I guess I was hoping it would be like the Malvado sisters and someone could bind his magic and the fae imprison him."

"The Malvados are gone?" Ruella's eyes sparkled. "I'm impressed. You must be insanely powerful to take them down. Someone needed to."

Before Addison could correct her, there was a

buzzing noise as Clarice came zooming into the room from under the door. Her pants and shirt were torn and her hair had gone flat. She definitely looked a little worse for wear. "There you guys are. When I said take off, I didn't mean far enough away. I'd have to take hours tracking you. Why are we even in here, and who is this?"

Addison cocked her head to the side. "Wait, you didn't see anyone in the big room with all the furniture?"

"Nope. It was empty. I did pass a house up top that had a bunch of things imprisoned, so I released all of them. Only two tried to bite me. I promised them I'd mcet them honorably on the battlefield and flew away." She plopped onto a rock jutting out of the wall so she was at eye level with them. "Who was I supposed to see?"

Addison felt more relaxed knowing Malachi was gone. "Malachi Darkwood was there. That was his house, and those were his prisoners."

Clarice giggled. "Oh, nice job finding him. When he gets back to an empty house, he is going to be so pissed. Now I kind of want to hide up there and wait for him to come back." She glanced over at Ruella. "And you made a friend? Even though I warned you not to talk to anyone."

She had a point. Not that Addison would admit that. "She saved us, okay? Her name is Ruella, and she's here hunting Malachi, too."

"Oh really. What did he do to you?" Clarice had serious trust issues.

"He destroyed my home and stole artifacts from us. He's collecting everything he needs to open a permanent door between this realm and the other realms. This will allow the darkness to spread and take over. I've been tracking him for a long time. He's leaving a wake of destruction behind him. I think the last place he needs is some metaphysical shop. There's a portal underneath that leads to a warehouse of forbidden magical artifacts."

"That's my friend's shop. He's threatening to destroy her store if she doesn't sell it to him." Everything made so much more sense now.

"No matter what, you can't let her sell to him. The fate of all realms depends on it." Ruella said solemnly. "I hope we can take care of him before anything happens to your friend's shop, but she absolutely can't sell."

Addison liked it better when her biggest problem was an eight-foot plastic flamingo. "This is bigger than us. We need to get out of here and regroup with the others. Ruella, you've been tracking him so you can easily get us back to this place, right?"

She nodded. "I can. We'll need someone to open and close portals." She looked expectantly at Clarice.

"Yes, yes. I'll help too." She looked put out, but secretly you could tell she loved being in the middle of everything.

"Wait. That means you can open a portal any time?" Addison glared at Clarice. The fae shrugged innocently. "There were a few times you could have opened one and saved us from any number of monsters."

Clarice looked genuinely confused. "Why would I do that? You signed the contract. You knew the rules. And you agreed to help with Malachi. You never asked me to open one for you."

"Forgive me for assuming you would act in our best interest without being asked to save us." Why was everything so difficult with Clarice? If this was how it was to work with all fae she would be happy to avoid them as much as possible.

Clarice gripped a stone pendant hanging around her neck and said something in her native language. A second later, a portal appeared on the wall. Unlike the one in the park that was icy and ominous, this one exuded warmth and friendliness.

She recognized those vibes. This was her portal home.

"If you'd all like to join me, we can gather the troops, make a plan, come back, and take that asshole down." She sounded much more confident than she felt. Thankfully, she had complete trust in Minnie, Luna, and Xavier. Surely they would know exactly what to do and would be so happy she found Malachi and unearthed his plan that they won't be pissed at her for going alone.

Right, and pigs can fly.

fourteen

ADDISON COULDN'T BELIEVE IT. When they stepped through the portal into her backyard, it was the middle of the afternoon and there was a flurry of activity inside the house. She could hear people arguing.

The magical occupants must have known the second the portal opened. Minnie and Luna stormed onto the back porch. Xavier, Theresa, her sons, and the ghosts right behind them.

Her heart warmed seeing them all there. Her circle of friends had grown so much in such a short time. She was grateful for each and every one of them.

"Where have you been?" Luna shouted.

"You have a lot of explaining to do." Minnie's

glare could make the bravest person shiver in fear.

"Don't send us away. We were worried." Francesca stood, wringing her hands.

"You're magic, not invincible." Xavier was the hardest to look at. He seemed disappointed.

It was like a punch to the gut. She never wanted to see that look from him ever again.

She whistled to get everyone to stop talking. "I'm sorry. I screwed up. I shouldn't have gone off on my own. I hadn't really meant for things to go as far as they did. I was going to have a look around-"

"A look around? You've been gone for almost two days." Minnie was livid.

Angry witch says what?

"It didn't feel that long there. There's no sun, so you can't tell time."

Theresa clapped her hands. "Enough airing your grievances out here for the whole neighborhood to hear. Let's get inside and find out who our new guests are."

The group grumbled as they filed back into the house. Addison stopped and kissed her mom's cheek. "Thank you."

"Don't thank me yet. I'm angry too. I'm letting everyone else say their peace first."

Crud.

Xavier stood in the kitchen and waited for her. He tucked a strand of hair behind her ear. A shiver ran down her back. She wanted to lean her head into his hand and feel him cup her face. She missed that intimate touch. Not that her husband had done it much in their marriage.

He pulled a leaf from her hair. "Are you okay? You look pretty beat up."

She glanced down and realized how badly her clothes had been torn. "All superficial. I'm really okay. Freaking starving, but okay."

Theresa closed the fridge door. "I'm already on it. I'll make sandwiches for you and your guests." She paused. "I assume that tiny thing was a fairy. Do they eat sandwiches?"

Addison opened her mouth to respond and realized she didn't know the answer. "Hang on. Clarice," she shouted.

"Yeah?" the tiny voice shouted back from the living room.

"Are you good with a peanut butter and jelly sandwich?"

The tiny fairy flew back into the kitchen. "If I accept food from you, you can't trap me here, right?"

Addison held her hands up. "My house is full

enough. I have no need to trap otherworldly beings here, too."

"In that case, I would love two PB&Js." She flew close to Addison and whispered. "Did you know you have a human and a ghost in love out there? They know that can't work, right?"

Addison sighed. "They know. That is a problem for another day, though."

"I wouldn't wait too long. They look like they are ready to make little Casper babies right now." With that, Clarice turned around and flew back into the living room.

Xavier stared after her. "She's an interesting character."

"You have no idea. Let's go sit. I'm pretty sure I haven't stopped moving since I went into the portal."

"Absolutely. I want a front-row seat to see if that tiny thing could actually eat two human-sized sandwiches." Xavier had a point. Did Clarice think they were fae-sized? They were about to find out.

The boys had dragged kitchen chairs into the living room and scattered them around so everyone could have a seat. Many more nights like this and she'd have to buy bigger couches. That was a great problem to have.

Theresa handed plates to Ruella and Addison while Leo set plates down for Nutmeg and Clarice.

Everyone watched as the fae flew down to the plate, sat on the crust, and dug in. It was impressive to watch.

"Okay. Fill us in." Minnie's arms crossed. She was clearly still pissed.

Addison held up her finger as she took large bites. In record time, she was done and wishing for more. She should be embarrassed to eat like that in front of Xavier but she made a promise to never be what a man wanted her to be. She was going to be her true, authentic self and they would accept her or not. Either way, it was no skin off her back.

A hiccup escaped her as she started to talk. "Excuse me. Okay, where do I start... I couldn't sleep, so I snuck off to the portal. That's where I met Clarice." She pointed at the fae who was already done with one sandwich and on to the next. Impressive. "She said she was hunting Malachi because he was trying to open a portal to the fae realm and she needed help. I thought about Luna and realized I could solve her problems if I teamed up with Clarice. While we were going over rules Nutmeg showed up, he'd been tipped off by the ghosts."

"Again, so sorry." Alexander shook his leg nervously.

If she could have patted his leg to calm him, she would have. "It's okay. You guys did what you thought was right. I'm glad Nutmeg was there with me. Anyway, we went through the portal, got chased a bunch, found Malachi's hideout-"

"Whoa, Whoa, Whoa. It was way more intense than you are making it sound. Let me,"

Ugh. Addison had been deliberately downplaying the danger.

Clarice brushed the crumbs off her clothes and flew to the center of the room. She waited until all eyes were on her. "With the hum of the potion in their veins, Addison and Nutmeg stepped through the portal. It was twilight, we couldn't see through the thick fog. Suddenly there were thundering footsteps coming at us,"

Addison sat back and closed her eyes. Clarice had a flare for the dramatics and was determined to put on a good show. She might as well catch a quick nap.

She was shaken awake by Xavier. "Now I see why you are so torn up."

Luna had her arms crossed, and she was glaring

at Addison. "I know your heart was in the right place, but don't you ever risk your life for me again. I can replace a shop. I can't replace you."

Addison blinked away tears.

"It's bigger than that, though," Ruella interjected. "He's threatening all the realms. We all have to put ourselves in danger to stop him."

Addison held her hand up. "Non-magic, non-supernatural people in the room excluded." As expected, her boys argued. She cut them off. "This is non-negotiable. I have magic and I don't know what I'm doing. You are amazing, brave men in your own right, but this isn't a fight you can win."

Minnie shrugged. "When we go fight Malachi, we could leave them at Luna's shop guarding the hidden portal. They can be a last line of defense and protectors of the human realm." She winked at Addison.

Next time they were alone, Addison was going to give Minnie a huge thank you. She gave the boys a way to feel useful, while also keeping them out of danger. With the wards set up at the shop, there would be no safer place for them. And this group wasn't going to let Malachi get anywhere near there.

"Okay, here's the plan," Luna took control. "I'm going to send Malachi a message that I'm considering his offer and that I need a few days to get things in order. That should buy us some time to teach Addison a few tricks. We'll stock up on supplies and go to his hideout. If we do our job right, he'll never leave the dark realm again."

Ruella held her hand up. "He has jump portals all through his cave system. We need to spread the word about what is happening and have everyone temporarily close every portal they can. We need to cut off his escape routes while we fight him. It needs to be perfectly timed, though. If the portals close too soon, he'll know something is up."

"Our coven can create a charm that will light up when it's time to close portals. It's just a matter of getting them everywhere they need to be in the next two days while also taming the chaos queen over here." Minnie always managed to have an insult ready to go.

"Hey now, I resemble that remark." She stuck her tongue out at her mentor. "Everyone knows what they need to do. The first step is getting out of my house so I can sleep for at least six hours. I need to call in sick at work too. Not sure how the boss will like hearing me say I'll be back in if I survive a magical battle."

"Maybe just say it's a family emergency." Theresa offered.

"Okay. I love you all, but if I see you before seven a.m. tomorrow I will try to purposely set you on fire." It was never good when she was sleep-deprived. She was all for saving the world... after a lengthy nap.

ADDISON SAT cross-legged on the couch. She felt fantastic. She'd slept for eight peaceful hours, took an extremely long, hot shower, and ate a bowl of cereal and two donuts. Now she was ready to learn.

Her cell phone sat on the coffee table in front of her. She focused on picturing the phone lifting up and levitating to her. How cool would that be?

Her brows drew together as she concentrated on the phone that hadn't budged in the two minutes she'd been trying. "Come on!"

The phone spun in a circle, shot into the air, and right into the hall mirror, shattering it.

"Well, now you've done it. That's seven years of bad luck. How have you not blown your house up yet?" Nutmeg sat on the fireplace mantle watching her with judgy eyes.

She laid her head back against the couch. "What's the use? I have to be the worst witch in the world."

"You said it, not me." She lifted her head and scowled at the groundhog. "Keep going, buddy. That dog carrier is in the other room."

Her face lit up as she felt Luna's energy coming up the driveway. She was almost back to her old self now that they had a plan.

Addison glanced at the front door. "Open." It swung open effortlessly, except for that annoying groan it had from her accidentally sending the couch hurtling against it. "See, I can do that magic effortlessly. What a useless power."

Luna announced herself as she walked in and closed the door. "Morning. You are looking much better."

Addison pretended to preen. "Thanks, it's effortless."

"Ha! I've seen your nighttime routine. More lotions and creams than any one person needs."

She wasn't too ladylike to hold her hand up and flick the groundhog off.

Luna tsked at them. "You are like children.

Before we do anything else, I think you should do the bonding ritual. Everything will be easier when you're connected."

Addison sneered. "I'm still not sure I want to bond with him. You heard him. He's mean to me."

"It's tough love, sweetheart," Nutmeg replied sweetly.

"Do me a favor, love me less." She shot back.

Luna aimed a spell at them, freezing them in place. Addison could breathe and move her eyes around, and that was it. "I've had enough of this. It's going to take everyone to stop Malachi. There are millions of people depending on us. We all know you guys are going to bond, so stop fighting it."

She dropped the spell. The look she gave them said if they were smart, they wouldn't complain she'd used magic on them. When she wanted to be, Luna could be scary.

Addison looked at Nutmeg. "She's right. I know we belong together and I know you'll make me a stronger, better witch. I'm ready if you are."

He opened his mouth, then closed it, then opened it again. He was likely going to say something sarcastic, but stopped himself. Smart. "I'm with the Schmidts forever. Let's do this."

Luna held up a bag. "I've got everything we need. Come on."

The trio made their way to the spare bedroom. As Addison had been delving more and more into the magic world, she was starting to collect a lot of stuff that the average human might question. After chatting with Nutmeg and finding out he actually felt calmer around magical artifacts, they decided to make his bedroom her witch's office as she liked to call it.

Luna handed Addison a bag of salt. "You are going to make one large circle with two overlapping circles inside it. The overlapping circles need to be big enough for you each to sit in."

Addison did as she was told while Luna saged the room and lit white candles.

When Luna was done, she pulled out a mortar and pestle. "A gift for you. This was one of my first sets. It would be an honor if you would use this when you are casting and creating."

"Awe," Addison squealed. "I am so grateful I found you when I did. I would be honored to have this."

"Great. Now put some of your nail clippings in there. You too, Nutmeg." Luna handed her a set of nail clippers. It was an odd request, but Addison had learned that every part of a being was important and could be used to strengthen a spell, so she didn't bother questioning her.

Nutmeg held a paw over the bowl and let Luna cut what she needed. She mixed them with several herbs and plants and ground them into dust. "Put the bowl in the section where your two circles over-lap. You'll know when it's time to light it on fire."

Addison couldn't hide her smile. Every time she was involved in real magic casting, it sent a thrill through her. These small glimpses were the reminder she needed saying it was all real. She really was a witch.

They got into position and faced each other. Luna guided them from a chair in the corner. "You are going to look into each other's eyes and sync your breathing. Take as long as you need. You'll know when the connection is complete. That's when you'll drop the match in the bowl as a final seal."

Addison nodded. "You ready Nutmeg?"

The groundhog nodded solemnly. "For all my pain in the ass ways, it really is my honor to serve you and your family."

She smiled at him. "Awe. I'm growing on you."

He rolled his eyes. "Can we do this already?"

Tough guy really struggled with his emotions. Good to see it was common in males of all species.

Everything outside the circles fell away as they focused on each other. At first, she didn't notice anything. When their breath clicked into sync, the air around them changed. It felt lighter, if that was even possible.

She felt her nipples tighten and knew her magic was working. A nearly invisible light burst from her chest and reached out to meet the same light coming from Nutmeg. They joined over the bowl, slithering like two snakes wrapping around each other until they merged to make one stream running in both directions. The air was knocked out of Addison when it happened. She saw Nutmeg take a gasping breath at the same time. All at once, she could clearly hear him in her head. She could feel everything he felt. Her magic had always been a light current of energy under her skin. Now she felt it in every cell of her being. The connection had amplified her power significantly.

Without breaking eye contact, she lit the match and dropped it in the bowl. There was a flash as the items immediately caught fire and burned out. When it was done, the light stream disappeared and the air in the room returned to normal. Luna was clapping in the corner. She'd forgotten the other witch was even in the room.

Luna looked wistfully at Addison and Nutmeg. "That was amazing. I'd never actually seen anyone do that ritual in person. I hope to have a familiar one day too."

Addison groaned as she got up off the ground. It was easier to do that when she was twenty years younger. "Why don't you have one now?"

"They come to us when we're ready. I've done rituals asking for my familiar to reveal itself. So far, nothing. I haven't given up hope, though. They'll find me when the time is right." She walked around, blowing out candles. "Next up, you need to cast a spell of protection on yourself."

Addison grabbed the piece of paper Luna held out and cleared her mind before reading the words. "By Earth and Air, By Fire and Water, so shall you hear my cell. Powers of Birth and Rebirth. Powers of Silence and Peace. Protect my body and mind."

Sparks flew from Addison's fingertips and rained down. Nutmeg squealed as his hair caught fire. He rolled frantically, trying to smother the embers.

Addison grabbed a vase of flowers, tossed the stems on the ground, and dumped the water on her poor familiar. He laid on his back, breathing heavily.

She bit her lip. "Not bad for my first time, right?"

Luna patted her back. "You said cell instead of call. It messed up your casting. It probably wouldn't have been a big deal, but now you are juiced up from your connection to Nutmeg."

Addison plopped onto the ground and scooped up her still smoldering familiar. "I'm truly sorry." She dug a crystal out of her pocket. "I worked with Minnie to imbue this with protection. I was going to give it to you before the big battle. Maybe you should hold on to it now."

He grabbed the crystal and hugged her. "I appreciate the gesture. Now if you'll excuse me, these clothes are ruined. I need to change."

Luna watched him leave the room before asking, "Are you making his clothes? He's quite fashionable."

"Right! I can't figure it out either." Addison chuckled to herself. Of course, she would have the only familiar who liked to dress up. Nothing was ever normal with her. And that was okay. She was happy with her weird and quirky life.

Now they just needed to survive Malachi so they could keep on enjoying it.

sixteen

ADDISON GRABBED the tray of cookies she'd stopped and bought and went inside *The Soul Apothecary*. Luna needed to open the shop, but they still had so much to do they decided to move Addison's training there. With the potential for her to do so much damage, she figured it was best to show up with goodies.

The shop was empty except for Luna and Clarice. They sat at the table in the back, arguing over something.

Addison set the cookies down and Clarice's eyes lit up. She flew over and pulled one off the plate and onto the table. She sat on it and started eating. Where did all the food go?

"So, what are we fighting over?" Addison asked.

"She's being unreasonable," Clarice mumbled with a full mouth.

"The fae would like to come in and find the portal for themselves and move the artifacts to their realm. There are a lot of problems with this. The biggest being they are witch artifacts, not fae. They just want to collect powerful items and keep them to themselves."

Clarice rolled her eyes, but didn't disagree with the accusation.

"I agree with Luna. If she didn't know the portal was here when she chose this spot for her shop, it means she was meant to be the caretaker." Addison was proud of herself. She'd been reading all about magic, fate, and destiny. There was so much that had happened in her life that she now believed was fate, not good or bad luck.

Clarice looked to Nutmeg, who had grabbed a cookie and sat next to her. "What about you? You're older than both of them."

With stuffed cheeks, he replied. "They're right. The fae don't need more power that doesn't belong to them."

The fairy shrugged and gave in. "Fine. When Malachi breaks in and steals it all, don't come crying to us."

Luna flipped open a book and slid it toward Addison. "If it gets to that point, we'll all be crying because that will mean he has everything he needs to open the portals to all the realms. And on that note, you can make this potion to help nullify Malachi's powers. The only bad part is it will require getting close enough to throw it on him."

"Let's worry about that when the time comes." She grabbed the book and took it over to the tall table where all of Luna's ingredients were shelved and a cauldron sat front and center. While the shop was open, there was a sign that said it was a replica of a witch's altar. The humans were none the wiser.

Nutmeg climbed onto the shelves and crossed the table. She glared at him. "Really? I don't think you actually packed that." He smiled at her from underneath a neon yellow hazmat suit, complete with a helmet and everything.

"Don't question magic." He sat on the edge of the cauldron, his legs dangling over the side. "Until you get the hang of things, I think this is the safest move for me. I still smell like burned hair."

"I said I was sorry." She read the directions of the potion three times and recited the words in her head to make sure she didn't mess up the words again.

When she felt confident, she pulled ingredients

and measured as the book described. She added the cayenne pepper, black pepper, garlic, rosemary, and black tourmaline. "What the heck is rue?"

"Look for it on the top shelf to the left. It's basically evergreen shrubs. Oh, and I got a new shipment of sealing wax in. Let me get the black wax for you." Luna disappeared into the back while Addison sifted through bottles.

"Man, she has a lot of stuff. I'm just glad it's not asking for eyeballs or anything slimy." She shuddered as she grabbed for the bottle of rue. The bottle next to it rocked and fell over. The contents rained down and right into the cauldron.

"Oh boy," was all Nutmeg got out before the potion bubbled violently, the table shaking from the force.

"Luna!" It was too late. Purple goo erupted from the cauldron and flew in every direction.

Addison had ducked down so most of the mixture had missed her. When she caught sight of Nutmeg, she couldn't hold back her laughter. His yellow hazmat suit was now grape colored. There wasn't an inch anywhere he wasn't covered. It was his fault really for sitting on the cauldron. He should have been smart like Clarice, who had stayed at the table. She was remarkably clean thanks to her quick thinking and hiding under a cookie.

A blob of the potion slid down Addison's forehead and dangled from her nose. It was going to take multiple showers to get it all out of her hair.

Luna came skidding out of the back room. She took in the sight of her beautiful shop that now looked like a crime scene where someone killed Barney and ran him through a grinder. "Oh Addison, you do make everything more interesting, don't you?" She stepped over puddles of purple goo and made it to the door, where she flipped the sign from open to closed. "Come on, Clarice, with your help I can have all this cleaned up in no time."

Clarice peeked around the cookie. "Oh, now you want the help of the fae?"

Addison sighed. "Clarice, please, do it for me. Remember, we're all on the same side."

She got up dramatically. "Fine. I expect double chocolate chip brownies in repayment. And none of that imitation American chocolate. I want the good stuff from Germany or Switzerland."

Who knew the fae were such connoisseurs of quality chocolate?

If she helped stop Malachi, Addison would feed her anything she asked for.

They were running out of time and Addison was still more menace than team member. She wasn't going to let it get her down. She had what it took to be a good witch, like every Addison that came before her. She just had 46 years of learning and practice to shove into two days. Easy, right?

seventeen

ADDISON FINISHED BRUSHING her teeth and was ready to climb into bed. It was still early, but running for your life through a dark realm for two days and then practicing magic for hours really took a lot out of a witch.

She reached for the light switch when she felt Xavier's energy coming toward her front door. It was vibrating faster than usual. Something was up.

She rushed to the front door and opened it as he stepped onto the porch. "I got a call from my sister. Her coven was getting in position to close portals, and they saw Malachi go through one. She followed him and saw him go through another portal. It disappeared before she could go through it. She did a locator spell on the off chance he was in our realm and it shows him at Luna's shop. I drove by there and it looks shut down."

"Luna is with the local coven assigning everyone to guard portals and they are reaching out to covens all over the world to do the same." She ran back to her room and grabbed her cell phone off the bedside table. At any other time, she'd be nervous about having Xavier standing in her bedroom. Now was not that time. She called Luna and when she didn't answer, she tried Minnie. "They must still be working. They don't carry their electronics while they're casting."

Xavier cursed. It was the first time she'd seen him not in 100% control of his emotions. "I assume you can get past Luna's wards and get into the shop?"

She nodded. "Of course. Give me two minutes to change."

"Sure."

She stared at him, waiting for him to catch on.

"Oh right, privacy. I'll be in the living room."

"Can you wake Nutmeg up and get him up to speed." She yelled out as he closed the door behind him.

If she was smarter and not on a time crunch, she should have started changing in front of him just to see his reaction. She thought he was interested in her. He wasn't the easiest person to read, though.

She tossed on her yoga pants and a sweatshirt. They were the cleanest clothes she had. She hadn't had time to exercise, so they hadn't seen much use.

Nutmeg was on Xavier's shoulder as they waited by the door for her. She rushed out behind them and climbed into Xavier's truck. Her heart pounded as they drove through the streets. Was Malachi nearby? Was he minutes away from destroying their world?

They pulled up to the store. As Xavier said, it was dark and undisturbed. She couldn't sense anyone in the store. The protection spell they cast over the shop was still in place. With Malachi, that didn't mean much.

She turned off the wards she needed to so Xavier could enter and used the alarm code Luna had given her in case of an emergency. The store was creepy at night. All the gothic decorations looked spooky in the dark.

Xavier led the way to the back room and down the basement stairs. The storage room was quiet. If Malachi had been there, he hadn't left a trace.

Xavier circled the room. "So, there is a secret entrance down here to a portal that leads to forbidden spells?"

"That's the rumor." The cinderblock walls didn't look impressive to her.

He ran his hand along one wall. "Can you sense anything?"

"Let me try." She sat down and closed her eyes. She focused on her breathing and entered a meditative state. Her nipples tightened as her magic woke up. For several minutes, there was nothing. Other than power signatures from items in the shop above, she wasn't sensing anything.

She gasped as a weight pushed against her chest. It was Nutmeg. She felt him the moment he connected with her. Magical signatures from further away were now in her awareness. Her right ear itched. She turned to scratch it and noticed the wall to her right was shimmering. It most definitely was not doing that before.

With one hand holding Nutmeg against her, she got up and walked over to the wall. The outline of a door faintly appeared inside the shimmer. "Holy shit. It's here."

Xavier ran over and felt every inch of the wall. He noticed a toolbox on a shelf and grabbed a hammer. "Back up."

Before she moved, she pointed. "This is the center of the door."

He swung hard and took a chunk out of the block she'd pointed at. Her stomach squirmed watching him. She had no idea it was so sexy to watch a man use a hammer. If he'd had his shirt off, she'd likely be panting right now. Thank god there was no shifter around. She'd read they could smell when a person was turned on. That was an unfair advantage, in her opinion.

As much as she was enjoying the show, it was taking too long. "Step back."

She concentrated on what she wanted to do and sent a surge of power at the wall. The blocks crumbled to bits, dust billowed around them.

She jumped into Xavier's arms and squealed. "I did it. I did a spell, and it didn't backfire."

"Nice job. I knew you could do it." He looked into her eyes as he leaned in. She was on a high from the magic. Screw her determination to keep him at arm's length. She leaned into meet him halfway when Nutmeg had to go and ruin it.

"Not for nothing, but we're on a time crunch here? Maybe you guys can table that for later?"

Addison really hoped he was reading her mind right now, so he'd know how pissed she was. The look of mischief in his eyes made it clear he absolutely knew.

Xavier cleared his throat as he stepped back from her. "Let's see what's behind door number one, shall we?"

Maybe she should thank Nutmeg for the distraction. She had to remind herself again not to lose her heart to Xavier. Fun flings only. She nodded and went to study the door. It was a plain old wooden door. Sure, it was well made, and the handle was old-fashioned, but there were no markings or anything to indicate something magical was hidden behind it.

Her hand shook from nerves as she reached out and turned the doorknob.

Nothing. It didn't budge. "Well, that was anti-climactic."

Xavier tried the handle and even threw his body against it a few times. That sucker wasn't moving.

"Why don't you just ask it to open?" Nutmeg offered.

"Come on, it wouldn't be that easy." She looked between Xavier and Nutmeg. Both shrugged. "Fine."

She focused on the door and what she wanted it to do. "Open."

Dust shimmered in the air as the door swung open silently.

Xavier laughed loudly. "I'll be damned. How did you know?"

Nutmeg shrugged. "It's pretty common for forbidden things to be accessible only to those who want them for selfless reasons. You guys have no intention of using anything in that room for a nefarious purpose. I figured it wouldn't hurt to see if the lore worked."

"After this, you deserve a whole new wardrobe, my treat. You may have just saved the day." She rubbed his head affectionately.

"I'm holding you to that," he shot back before jumping to the ground and running through the door.

A loud rumble followed by a whoosh of dirt and debris flew at them. "Nutmeg!" Addison's heart was in her throat. The area behind the door had collapsed. Why did he think it was okay to rush in?

She dropped to her knees and dragged pieces of the rubble away. Xavier was next to her, moving twice as fast. Tears stung her eyes, but she wasn't going to give in. She would feel it if Nutmeg was dead. He couldn't be.

Her fingers were raw by the time a flash of yellow material appeared in the dirt. Xavier brushed away the area while Addison pulled Nutmeg free.

"Come on, buddy. Take a breath." She held her hand over his chest and sent her power into him.

He took a huge gasping breath as he sat up. "What happened?"

"You scared the shit out of me, is what happened. It was booby-trapped. You're lucky you're alive or I would have killed you myself." Damn groundhog had taken ten years off her life. He may be a pain in the ass, but he was her pain in the ass. She set him down on a nearby shelf. "Stay there while we clear the area."

She wished she knew a spell to move the rubble. Xavier didn't complain. He took his jacket off and started digging.

Slowly, they made progress.

He stopped to wipe sweat from his brow. "Maybe later you can tell me what Nutmeg meant about me and a watermelon?"

Her jaw dropped open. She was going to have groundhog soup for dinner. How did she get out of this one? Did she want to get out it? "Dreams can be interpreted a lot of different ways. I'm not even sure where he was going with that." Ugh, why did she lie?

He looked almost disappointed. "I see. No matter, we need to get back to work anyway."

Why was she so stupid around him?

They went back to working in silence. Eventually, they could see more. The door led to a hallway and only the first few feet had caved in. Now that Addison had a minute, she studied the area. "If there was a magic spell on this hall, I think it broke when Nutmeg set it off. I don't sense anything else except something at the very end. We'll have to get closer though, so I can see it better."

"Take it slow." For being non-magical, he sure wasn't afraid to stand shoulder to shoulder with her as they crept down the passageway.

The air was musty and tickled her nose. No one had been down there in a long time. When they reached the end, she realized she was looking at a portal. It was different from the one in the park. This one was blue, and the mist moved like waves on the ocean. It was beautiful to watch. She brushed her hands across it. There was no malice or iciness like the other portal, either. "I think it's okay. I'll go first."

Xavier grabbed her arm to stop her. "Be careful. If anything feels off, come right back."

The concern in his eyes was heartwarming.

She took a deep breath and walked forward with her hands out. The portal didn't resist as she stepped through. On the other side was a large room with rows and rows of shelves. Each one was stuffed full of objects radiating magic. A bookshelf along the back wall was filled with books of all shapes and sizes.

Addison stopped suddenly, Xavier bumping into her back. She held her hand up to silence him. Something moved in the far corner. They bent low and crept around the aisles until they could get a clear view.

"Well, shit."

Sitting at a desk flipping through a book was Malachi Darkwood. A portal that felt like the one in the park was open next to him. He'd beat them to the forbidden room. Were they too late?

She refused to believe it. There was no way she was letting him win. Not if she, her non-magical, non-boyfriend, and her groundhog had anything to say about it.

eighteen

"WHAT ARE WE DOING?" Addison, Xavier, and Nutmeg were startled as someone whispered behind them. Luna stood crouched next to them.

Addison waved her back through the portal. She took a deep breath when they were back in the hall-way. "How did you find us?"

"I got here to open the store and noticed my alarm was off. I was checking things out and saw the huge hole in my wall. Thanks for that by the way. I followed it and found the portal. I figured either you or Malachi had gone through, so I took a chance."

Addison cocked her head to the side. "Why are you opening the store in the middle of the night?"

Luna squinted her eyes at her. "Check your phone. It's almost eight in the morning. How long have you guys been here?"

"I got to Addison's around eleven last night," Xavier answered. "I guess it took longer than we thought to knock down the wall and dig our way to the portal."

Now that she knew what time it was, she let out a long yawn. "I'd love to go take a nap right now. Unfortunately, Malachi is in there. We need a game plan."

Luna's jaw dropped. "What? I didn't even see him. I was so focused on you guys. Let's get back in there."

Addison grabbed Luna's arm to stop her. "You're ready to take him on right now?"

Before she could answer, Malachi appeared through the portal. He stopped, stunned to see them standing there. He darted back inside.

Well, shit. They had no choice now.

One after another, they ran through the portal. Beams of light were flying across the room as Malachi sent spells over his shoulder. A shelf with boxes of bones on it was hit. Like a horror movie, the bones came to life and formed into skeletons. Xavier grabbed a sword off the wall. "I got them. You guys take care of Malachi."

A blast of wind shot down one of the aisles shoving Addison against a wall. Nutmeg was flung in the air and sent across the room. Luna had ducked and rolled. She shot back to her feet and kept running. She lobbed spells at Malachi. One hit him in the ass. His howl of pain was music to Addison's ears. Tired of fighting against the wind, she screamed stop and magically it did.

Nice.

A shelf full of mummified butterflies came to life and flew at Luna. She went running down an aisle to escape them.

Addison saw the lit candle on the table where Malachi had been sitting and remembered back to when Minnie had her practicing with the elements. She repeated what she'd done that day and, as expected, a giant flame blazed from the candle and straight at Malachi. He used his cloak to block the worst of it.

"Enough you chits." He roared at her.

Who the hell still uses the word chit? Were they in the 1800s?

Luna slid to a stop next to Addison. "Did he just call us chits?"

"Right?" What a weirdo.

Malachi flung a bottle at them. An invisible barrier encompassed them. They couldn't move. "Let me finish what I'm doing and I'll be on my way. When my spell is in place, you'll get what's coming to you."

He turned and made his way back toward the portal.

Luna glanced at the table and read the page of the book that was laid open. "Nutmeg." She whispered. The groundhog appeared around the corner. "I know what he's looking for. I need you to go up to my store and go to my supply area. There is a box of crystals and stones on the lowest shelf. Find the stone that is purple with gold and silver lines running through it. Get it and bring it back to us. Don't let him see you."

Nutmeg took off and stayed along the wall. Addison had to hope he'd make it unnoticed. She didn't want him facing Malachi on his own.

Xavier finally made his way back to them. "Skeletons are surprisingly good fighters. That was intense. What's going on with you guys?"

Luna took a deep breath and blew out a breath. The barrier around them disintegrated. "I was letting Malachi think he'd trapped us. He's on his way up to the shop. He's looking for a stone I sent Nutmeg for. We need to slow Malachi down."

Xavier didn't hesitate. He lifted his sword and took off toward the portal.

"Wait, you should really let the witches lead the attack," Luna yelled after him.

They caught up to Malachi as he was about to step through the portal.

"You didn't think you stopped us, did you?" Luna had sass, that was for sure.

The dark wizard spun around, veins throbbing at his temples. "This will all be over soon. You're too late."

Luna tapped her chin thoughtfully. "You're not looking for the stone of Alazir are you?"

Malachi's face went slack. "What, how?"

"You won't find it here. As soon as I figured out what it was, I sent it far away. It's somewhere I can't even reach now." Addison didn't want to play poker with Luna. She was excellent at bluffing.

Rage contorted Malachi's face. He roared as a wave of power blasted from him, sending them flying backward.

Out of the corner of her eye, she saw Xavier's head hit the stone wall, and he dropped to the ground, unconscious.

Oh no Malachi did not just hurt her fantasy boyfriend. She'd had enough of this wizard and his temper tantrum.

nineteen

ANGER COURSED through Addison's veins. She was seeing red. It was never good to cast when your emotions were high. She had no choice.

Malachi sent spell after spell at her. She deflected them with ease. Don't ask her how. She had no clue. Maybe the past Addison's were helping.

One of the deflected spells headed straight for Luna, who was still dazed from being blasted. Addison sent a shield up and smiled when it deflected the curse. Unfortunately, her attention had been off Malachi long enough for him to send a pile of dragon scales flying at her. Several of them sliced her with their razor-thin edges. It burned like fire, but none of them were deep enough to cause a problem.

She pictured the scales turning back and forming a shell around him.

It was pure shock to see them do as she intended. Malachi could be heard screaming from within the cocoon of scales.

She ran over to Luna and made sure she was okay, and then went to Xavier. He was unconscious but breathing. It was better he was out of the fight anyway.

"Now, what do we do with him?"

Luna just had to ask.

A cracking sound echoed around the room for a few seconds before the scales shattered into dust. Malachi roared at them. "I've had enough of you two." He raised his arm, murder in his eyes.

Addison was desperate. She called on her ancestors to help her as she cast a spell of protection around them and the store.

Loud cawing noises came rushing in through the portal seconds before hundreds of birds came flying in. They flew right toward Malachi. Feathers floated around the room as something screeched. It was hard to tell if it was Malachi or the birds.

The noise stopped as the birds flew back through the portal. All that was left behind was an unconscious Malachi. His clothes were shredded, and cuts crisscrossed his body.

Nutmeg came running back through the portal. "Did you guys see all those birds? That was crazy." He held the stone up to Luna. "You got a customer up there. It's Augie, and she wants to speak to the manager."

"She spoke to you?" How was the old biddy not freaking out?

He gave her a bored look. "Really? You told me humans shouldn't see me. She was muttering to herself as she paced the store."

Xavier groaned as he sat up. "What'd I miss?" He caught sight of Malachi. "Woah, what did you guys do to him?"

The dark wizard sat up so fast he made everyone jump. Luna and Addison braced for a magical attack.

Malachi's face turned from rage to disbelief to terror. "What have you done?"

Addison and Luna exchanged glances. "Could you be more specific?" Addison asked.

"It's gone. You took it." He stood up and flailed his arms as he rattled off hexes.

"Awe, is someone impotent?" Luna laughed loudly.

It took Addison a minute to catch up. "Your

magic, it's gone?" How the hell had the birds done that? It certainly hadn't been her intent. Not that she minded in the least.

Malachi dropped to his knees. "Please, give me back my magic and I'll go away. You'll never see me again." She actually felt bad for him. He was terrified. "Please, I'm nothing without my magic."

"That's exactly why you need to lose it," Minnie said snidely as she waltzed through the portal with Clarice sitting on her shoulder. "You've caused enough trouble. I've been up all night closing portals because of you. Do you see the bags under my eyes? Beauty like this doesn't come effortlessly."

Addison shook her head at the witch. "Oh my god, Minnie. You always know how to lighten the mood."

"I, for one, can't wait to see how he does living like a mortal in the suburbs." Nutmeg offered from his perch on a shelf filled with bottles of glowing liquid.

Xavier shook his head. "No way. We can't let him loose. He knows enough magic to always be a danger."

"So, what do we do with him?" Addison certainly didn't want him in her neighborhood. One crazy person was enough.

A loud pop got everyone's attention. Malachi was gone.

"Fuck. Where did he go?" Xavier growled.

"Relax. I took care of him." Clarice said cheerfully.

"What do you mean you took care of him? Did you kill him?"

She rolled her eyes. "Of course not. That would take too much paperwork. He's behind bars in the fae realm."

Nutmeg snorted. "Sure he is. You expect us to believe that?"

She scowled at the groundhog. "I'd be happy to send you there to see for yourself."

Nutmeg shook his head quickly. "Nah, I'm good. I believe you."

"Excellent. Now, who's buying breakfast?" The forever hungry fae asked the room.

Addison loved this quirky group. They were everything she never knew she needed in her life. "Why don't we go back to my house? I'll call my mom and the boys over. We'll have a big brunch and then we can all sleep for a few days."

Clarice opened a portal. "Lead the way."

Addison poked her head through the portal and then stepped back. "You can open a portal right into my living room? That seems like an invasion of privacy."

Minnie patted her on the back. "The fae don't know the meaning of privacy. Don't worry, I'll help you set up a ward so she can't do it again."

Clarice folded her arms and pouted. "You guys are no fun."

Addison shook her head and led the way through the portal. Once again, her house was full and she loved it.

ADDISON ZIPPED HER SUITCASE CLOSED. It was the last bag she had to pack before heading to the airport. The Schmidties were heading to Scotland. Now that things had quieted down, she wanted to know more about her birth family. Nutmeg was sure there was still an aunt alive in the Highlands and her mother's house was likely still being cared for since it was a family home.

Addison was finally going to get answers. She was going to see the place where she was born and walk the same halls her mother did. Secretly, she hoped she'd find a hint that her mother was still alive. She knew it was wishful thinking.

Fitz, Iggy, and Leo were in the living room talking to the Schmidties while they waited for her.

She had been a little hesitant to include Minnie on the trip since she was never really sure if the witch liked her or not. In the end, she was a part of the team and a nice distraction when Xavier and Luna got snippy with each other. They had gotten much more tolerant, but there were still times they slid back into their old ways of insulting the other.

She did a double-take when she saw the small dog curled up on the couch. Then she remembered Minnie had spelled Nutmeg so they could bring him on the flight as a service animal.

Luna was thrilled to go on the trip. She'd never been out of the country before. A few of the witches in the coven had volunteered to run her shop while they were gone, so she wouldn't lose business.

Xavier had a brother who lived in Spain. He was going to come to Scotland while they were there. She couldn't wait to meet the magical side of Xavier's family. She hoped some point soon he'd open up to her about why he was the only one without powers. What she really wanted to know was how they all treated him. Was he the black sheep of the family? Was he pitied? He stood by the couch talking to Theresa. His three-piece suit was without a wrinkle in it. This man was no black sheep and not a person to be pitied.

Even Alexander was coming along. He had never been out of the country when he was alive. Plus, he would keep Nutmeg busy with their long talks about poetry. Win-win for everyone.

"Remind me again why we can't have Clarice open a portal for us?" Minnie asked for the tenth time.

"Because she's still in trouble for sending Malachi there without warning. He's been a whiny mess since he arrived, and the fae are ready to kill him." Addison had felt bad when she heard Clarice was in hot water with her clan. Everyone liked to remind her that Clarice chose to send him to the fae realm. No one had asked her to do that.

Theresa noticed Addison standing in the doorway. She walked up and hugged her. Addison held on a little longer than normal. "You sure you're okay with me going?"

Theresa cupped her cheek. "You need to learn your history. I'm not going anywhere. You're stuck with me."

Addison pulled her into another hug. "I wouldn't want it any other way."

Leo and Francesca stood in the corner having a heated discussion. Several times they glanced at Addison. It was time she forced them to talk to her.

She walked over and smiled. "I can tell you guys are cooking something up. What is it?"

Leo straightened his shoulders. "Well, we've been doing some research, and we heard about a Necromancer in the Northeast who has had luck putting ghosts back in living bodies." The room went silent as every person, groundhog, and ghost turned to look at him. "Her name is Ava. We heard she's done it a couple of times already with success. If it's okay, we'd like to go see her while you're gone. We don't know if she'd be willing to help us, but we have to try."

Addison couldn't ignore the adoration on Francesca's face as she looked up at Leo. They really were in love. She would never deny any of her sons from being with the person they loved. "Absolutely, you should reach out to her. Please don't do anything though until I return. I'd like to meet her first and make sure everything is on the up and up. Francesa may be new to our family, but that doesn't mean I won't watch out for her like I would any of you."

"If I could hug you, I would." Francesca bounced on her toes. "Maybe in a couple of months, I'll be able to!"

Addison's phone chimed. It was her reminder to

leave for the airport. "Okay Schmidties, time to move out. Fitz, thanks again for taking us to the airport."

He gave her a mock salute. "Serenity's SUV is huge, so not a problem."

"I'm still bummed you haven't brought her over yet. Are you scared to let her meet me?"

He waved his hand around the room at the eclectic group. "This will be a lot to explain."

Addison chuckled and nodded her head. "Good point. Take as much time as you need."

The noise level picked up again as everyone grabbed a bag and headed outside. She still couldn't believe this was her life now. Thank goodness for divorce and perimenopause or she'd never have found this crazy bunch. That would have been the biggest travesty of all. She would tolerate a few hexes and hijinks if it meant getting to be with her makeshift family.

Chaos and Courtship - Book 3 in the Addison Schmidt Chronicles releases on August 13th, 2024.

Life's been anything but ordinary for Addison Schmidt, a witch with a talent for attracting trouble. But when an ancient magical force threatens to plunge the world into darkness, Addison finds herself chosen as the unlikely hero.

With reality blurring and chaos looming, Addison relies on her wit, resilience, and a quirky band of companions to navigate the paranormal challenges ahead. As she battles monsters, unravels mysteries, and confronts midlife, Addison embarks on a wild ride through a supernatural funhouse.

She'll go on an epic journey of magical misadventures, where laughter reigns and snark is the second language. Can Addison save the day and uncover the secrets of the ancient being? There's only one way to find out, and it's bound to be a wickedly good time.

Cassidy and her family recently relocated to the North Georgia Mountains after a lifetime in the Tampa Bay, Florida area. She's on a new adventure and loving every minute of it.

She loves reading and going to the movies, but not nearly as much as she enjoys traveling and hopes to one day watch a baseball game in every MLB stadium in the country.

She also writes under the pen name C.K. O'Connor. Books by C.K. range from sweet romance to young adult to historical romance.

To learn more about C.K. / Cassidy please visit her online at

www.cassidykoconnor.com.

You can also find her on Facebook at

https://www.facebook.com/CK-OConnor-Author-101376192171379

OR

www.facebook.com/cassidykoconnorauthor

<u>Paranormal Investigative Services Series</u>

Faeted under Fire

Stitched Under Fire

Taken Under Fire

Nightshade Guild Series

Mated To A Mage

Magic Burned

Swing Time

Crimson Moon Hideaway

Bearly Healed

The Fast and The Furry

Love Possessed

<u>Black Hollow Series</u>

Loving the Monster Within

Reviving Love

Sacrificing Love

Accepting Love

Resisting Love

Mending Love

<u>Forgiving Love</u>

<u>Fearing Love</u>

<u>Stand Alones</u>

Gruff Love

Sexy In White

To Steal a Prince's Heart

Wicked Wonderland Retreat Box Set